YOU'RE ALWAYS WELCOME...
AT THE BLOODRIDGE MOTEL

To My Parents,

Who allowed me to watch horror films at a very
impressionable age.

J. HUNTER RICHARDSON

YOU'RE ALWAYS WELCOME... AT THE BLOODRIDGE MOTEL

O.S.O.A.

You're always welcome. That was the sign hung outside the Bloodridge Motel, an establishment my family had owned for generations. Located atop a mountain named for the red jasper deposits found near its peaks, the motel was a relic from the heyday of Route 66. Nestled among large pines off a two-lane mountain road, it was built as a bungalow-style rest stop serving as a respite for road-weary travelers and families in need of sleep. The rooms were plain and practical but had a coziness to them. The motel predated novelty architecture like the tee-pees and train cars of the '30s and '40s. We were the only place to sleep for fifty miles in either direction, making it a necessary stop for those long-haul road trips.

My family, like the motel itself, seemed to exist in a world that time had forgotten. My mother, father, older sister, and I didn't have much, but at least we had each other. We were always about a decade behind the rest of the world in terms of pop culture and technology. At one point, the décor in the motel had become so outdated it came back around to being in style again. Postmodern retro chic, one review called us—my mother printed that one out and hung it in the lobby. When the Internet was installed so that we could take online reservations, it seemed as though the modern world had finally knocked at our door. If not for that small connection to the outside world, I'm not sure I could have survived high school. Still, our lone computer remained in the lobby and lived there years past being obsolete. Motel necessities, like new bed sheets, appliances, or a working thermostat, always took priority over technology. Even the televisions in each room never evolved past bulky tube sets, no matter that it wouldn't have cost much to replace them.

"If it ain't broke, why fix it?" was my father's favorite phrase—the irony being that he seemed to love fixing things. Rarely in the office, he could be found out back, behind the motel in his denim coveralls, and carting around his large toolbox, always in search of the next project. He worked hard his whole life, so even in his twenties he appeared to be around middle age. His wrinkles formed early and only deepened as he got older. Becoming a father at the age of forty certainly didn't help either. Still, there was always a kindness in his eyes and he took pride in the fact that people chose our motel to stay the night.

My mother, on the other hand, seemed to harbor a bit of resentment toward the life she inherited through marriage. She never outwardly complained, but her feelings were more than obvious when she would ruminate on the potential she had displayed in high school theater. Only knowing her as a reserved, professional adult, I found it hard to picture her as an outgoing performer. I do recall, when I was much much younger, hearing her sing when she thought she was alone. I guess in a way, for her, every visitor was an audience and every smile and enthusiastic greeting was a performance. Even though they may have been superficial, I could say for certain that she treasured every interaction. There weren't a lot of other families nearby, so there weren't a lot of opportunities for friendship, for any of us really. Loneliness was so ingrained in our being that I didn't even recognize it for many years.

When I was old enough to grasp the difficulty of our isolated life, I once asked my father, "Why don't we live with everybody else?"

"Because people need us to be here. If we weren't here to help, they would have nowhere to go. The mountain would be a dangerous place without us," he explained. The way he said it made me think he was repeating the explanation his father gave to him. The responsibility of owning this remote motel was not lost on me. But I didn't understand why that responsibility fell on us.

"Why can't somebody else do it?" I asked, envious of the kids at school who would make plans to see their friends on the weekends.

With a heavy sigh that betrayed his own conviction, he said, "Your grandpa sacrificed a lot to make a life for our family up here. It's only right that we honor that sacrifice and keep his dream alive."

According to family legend, my grandfather was a smart man and perpetually opportunistic to boot. When the nearby cave system was incorporated into the National Park Service, he capitalized on it by building the motel as close to it as possible. Situated on a small plot sitting smack dab on the border of a national park, the motel was surrounded by protected land.

That naked plot was an isolated island of commercial possibility for anyone daring enough to have a vision. Sitting at the edge of a dozen disjointed acres, the motel inhabited a relatively small footprint of our land. Miles away from the nearest town, our family home was built next to it, on the same plot. As tourism grew, so did the motel, one room at a time, gobbling up every inch of available land. Once the landlocked motel had nowhere else to go, it turned inward, cannibalizing parts of our house. It didn't take long before our old living room was converted into the motel office, with the door behind the lobby desk leading directly into our kitchen. Eventually, our home and the motel became one and the same. It was an architectural chimera of personal and professional life, inhabited by my family for nearly a hundred years. With a revolving door of faceless travelers and road-worn salesmen, the motel served as an oasis for wanderers. Always a last resort for the desperate. It was strange and sad, the last stop for miles and the only option for rest. The motel was a black hole of desperation and, for better or worse, it was where I grew up.

My dad was also raised in this isolated motel, disconnected from normal society. My mother always said that despite what he preached about honor and duty, he was hesitant to force the same fate on us. When my grandfather died suddenly, it was less of a choice and more of fate forcing itself on my father. I have memories of him talking about selling it, but that idea seemed to fade as we settled in as a family. Things appeared to go well for us, for a while at least.

I remember that part of my childhood fondly. We lived in a place that seemed only to be described in fantasy books. My sister and I would play in the woods and explore the untouched lands of the national park surrounding us. Around the motel, there were certain places we were told not to go, sections of the property that were off limits for one reason or another, but outside of our property, it was all fair game. While the park had the biggest caves and the truly impressive caverns, there were other hidden gems of natural wonder all around us. As kids, we had a kinetic sense of adventure and danger was only present in hindsight. My sister may have been older than me, but she wasn't any less adventurous. More than once we came face to face with death and brushed it off like nothing more than a scraped knee. Sinkholes, cave-ins, and ferocious wildlife were so common that caution came as an afterthought.

Thinking back on it, I sometimes wonder how I survived to adulthood. The caves alone were a death trap, too dangerous for the public but remote enough to not require warning signs. These were our favorite places to play. I always enjoyed how the cave chambers would echo when a heavy wind would come through. Sometimes, if you listened closely, it sounded as if they were calling your name, begging you to climb inside and explore. On occasion, my sister and I would give in to that beckoning call, but when we did, we never remembered flashlights. We were fearless.

Other times we would wander down to the park's welcome center, where we enjoyed free admission as cute kids and the only locals for miles around. I spent hours there reading about the lives of people who first explored the cave system, wishing I could meet them but knowing they were all long dead. The rangers who worked there paid little mind to us, letting us roam freely until my mother inevitably called and asked them to send us home. We spent so much time there as children, yet after a point, I went decades before stepping foot in the welcome center again. Still, as a child, it was the closest thing we had to a theme park, and we loved it. I must have ridden the elevator down to the subterranean caverns over a hundred times with my sister. Those were the good old days.

Unfortunately, shortly after my sister's 9th birthday, she got sick. The doctors in the city wanted to see her often and it wasn't easy for my parents to get down the mountain in our old, tired truck, but a week before her 10th birthday, she was diagnosed with a rare form of Leukemia. We didn't spend a lot of time outside together after that; in fact, she didn't spend a lot of time outside of her room. Everything happened so quickly, it wasn't long before the disease left her gaunt and almost unrecognizable. I didn't like being around her looking like that, so I did my best to avoid her. At the time, I didn't understand the seriousness of her disease. Instead, I went out and explored on my own, without her. Whether it was ignorance or denial, nothing changes the fact that I abandoned her.

I don't remember her death, but I do remember the weeks leading up to it. When the doctors informed my parents that nothing more could be done, they insisted on bringing her back, back to the motel, back to her room. They set up machines and other medical stuff in there to help ease the pain. The syncopated beeps and wheezing respirator bled through the walls in audible misery. In those moments my chest would tighten and I couldn't breathe, as every one of her breaths sounded like the last. It pained me to see her in that state. I was so young, I didn't know how to process it all, so I would leave to go exploring without her. In my head, this was temporary; like every other sickness, we always got better. She would get better. All I needed was to be patient and everything would work out.

I wasn't there when she died. My parents had sent me to my aunt's for a few weeks. Looking back now, I understand why. Before then, I had never been on a trip without my parents or sister. In the days I spent away from them, I was so caught up in being the center of attention, I thought very little about my sister and her illness. I think that was the point. I don't remember much, but I do recall my Aunt Carol showing me so much affection that it seemed foreign. I didn't understand at the time, but it was clear in retrospect that she pitied me. It was as if her every action were guided by guilt. From the ice cream sundaes to the extra-long bedtime stories, she went above and beyond, taking care to make sure I knew I was loved. It would have been one of the best times of my life, but afterward, the stain of my sister's death tainted every memory.

When I returned, my sister was gone.

My mother didn't take her death well. Tortured by any reminder of my sister's sickness, she experienced a complete mental breakdown and insisted my sister be erased from our home. My sister's room was cleared of her bed and those awful, noisy machines. It was converted into storage for various motel amenities, swallowed up like the rest of our house.

Unwilling to even donate her old things, my mother resorted to torching my sister's clothes and toys in a large burn pit at the furthest reaches of our property—all without regard for me or my own grieving process. If I wanted a keepsake, an old dress, or even a blanket, something to remember my sister by, well, that was just too bad.

Soon after, I wasn't even allowed to say her name. Every day there was less and less evidence that my sister had ever lived with us. Eventually, my mother went so far as to rid the house of any photos of her. One by one, they were cropped to remove my sister. By the time I was a teenager, there was no trace of her existence. I hate to admit it, but even my memory of her face had faded. She became nothing more than a faceless, fuzzy silhouette framed by frizzy hair. I still remembered one thing about her. I remembered she smelled like soft lavender.

High school was my first real escape from the isolation of home. There were enough homesteads up on the mountain that a bus stop was established in the vicinity. It was still a half-hour drive from our home and another forty-five minutes once I got on the bus. Despite the commute, my parents decided it would be good for me to be around others my age. Luckily the only other kid on the bus was in my grade; a skinny, blonde boy named Graham Nellis, whose family also lived in near isolation.

Graham's father was a park ranger, as was his grandfather. They had established a family legacy of watching over the cave system and surrounding woods. Because of this, Graham's family had been allowed to build a home on a specific plot of land. Our families were more acquaintances than friends, but it was always understood that we could call on each other in an emergency. More than once we kids had been dumped at each other's homes while our parents attended to some urgent matter down the mountain. While Graham and I became friends by default, our connection wasn't strong enough to survive the social cliques of a high school campus.

I drifted towards the more interesting kids, addicted to living vicariously through their mundane yet fascinating lives. Their stories about trips to the video rental store were as thrilling as the films they rented. Graham's life was too similar to mine to provide any sort of fantasy. By the end of senior year, though we barely spoke, Graham offered to start driving me to school after he was given his father's truck for his 18th birthday. For those last two months, Graham and I reconnected on the drive down the mountain. But, like most high school relationships, graduation day was the last time I saw him for years.

After graduation, I left the motel and went to college, living my own exciting yet uneventful life, far away from that small spot on the mountain. I made friends, loved partners, and felt the pain of loss as college relationships crumbled with the distance of real life. As people moved home or embarked on their adulthood journeys, we lost touch. I did my best to hold onto the exciting city life that college had gifted me, but as my parents grew older, they needed more help. Weighted by the guilt of abandoning them, I felt drawn back to that old mountain motel, so back I went to the life I had left.

Relinquishing all hope of an independent life, I ended up "helping" them for a good part of twelve years. Slowly, I took on more and more of the responsibilities until I pretty much ran the place myself. I absorbed and took on every aspect, from cleaning to bookkeeping, and as my parents grew older, I matured. As their abilities faded, I became more capable. On one chilly December morning, after I cleaned the rooms and checked out the guests, I realized that I was in charge.

My parents still insisted on certain tasks, of course, odd things that they were not ready to give up. I imagine they still needed a sense of worth. They still tended to the "legacy" guests—families who stayed with us as a tradition, or guests who evolved into old friends from repeat stays. My parents enjoyed helping them, and that was fine with me. Most were older anyway, and the less time I had to spend pretending to catch up, the better. Some of these guests had quirky requests that, for one reason or another, my parents went out of their way to fulfill.

For instance, we had an entire box of black charcoal soap. We only used it for one old woman who had been staying with us for years, stopping on her way to and from seeing her son the next state over. The box of soap was purchased in 1973 and one bar at a time it dwindled, but somehow it outlasted the old woman. On her last visit, she explained that her son was moving and she no longer felt up to the long drives. My father tried to give her the remaining soap, but she didn't have space in her trunk. So it lived in my sister's old room, waiting for another special request.

Specific thread-count sheets, certain toilet paper, or special chocolates left on a pillow were a few of the more mild requests. Over years of watching my parents struggle to meet the guest's needs, I realized one specific truth... The stranger the request, the stranger the guest behind it.

The strangest of all involved a group of guests that I had come to call The Family. They consisted of seven members: an older couple, a middle aged couple, two teenagers (a girl and a boy), and a younger girl around the age of 11. My memories of them stretch back to my earliest memories of the motel. They always stuck out because my parents treated them differently.

For as long as I could remember they had visited us every two years like clockwork. The seven of them were always polite, and quiet, and never stayed for less than a week. My parents had even circled the date on our calendars, always expecting them. My father made sure to have the same room open, even though they never seemed to book ahead. They were almost like old friends, except for the fact that they treated us like strangers every visit. It wasn't like they didn't remember us, but more that we were inconsequential in their lives. We were staff, only there to meet their needs and any small talk was either of the matter at hand, or unimportant. The interactions were so brief and infrequent that if it weren't for one odd thing, I doubt I'd have remembered them. It hung over my head, never explained, and never acknowledged by my parents. I just accepted it as an open secret that for some reason, we all agreed to keep.

From their looks alone, they seemed painfully ordinary, but this family I had known for my entire life were unlike anyone else I had ever encountered on the mountain or below. Despite watching me grow from an infant into a fully functioning adult, trained to serve them for one week every other year. Despite years of impeccable, unquestion-ing service, and everything I know about the laws of nature and the universe.

Despite it all, I ignored the fact that throughout my entire life, The Family, themselves, never seemed to age.

The Family came every odd year like clockwork, never missing a visit. There were several times before moving back, though, that I missed them, especially after my sister died. My parents would send me to stay with my Aunt Carol for a bit and it always seemed to coincide with their visit. Sometimes, I would arrive back home just as they left, only catching a glimpse of their packed car pulling out of the parking lot. At one point, I had gone over a decade having only seen them through those dusty old car windows. Still, even though the dirt and grime of the glass, I could tell their faces remained the same.

Those wonderful week-long visits with my aunt were filled with love and attention that was still very much lacking from my home life. I looked forward to these trips, which sometimes fell in between The Family's visits, but always, without fail, on them. It was in my teenage years I began to realize the attention I received from my aunt came from a place of pity rather than familial love. I never complained though. I drank it in and held onto it knowing full well that in the weeks after I returned— the weeks after The Family's visits—my mother was always at her most distant. She was colder, more disconnected, and visibly distraught. Even in the later years, when I came back to live at home again, this trend continued. There was something about this odd, ageless Family that took its toll on her emotionally.

Unfortunately, those trips to my Aunt Carol's ceased when she had a falling out with my mother. In the years I was living on my own, I had tried to reach out to her, but those calls were rarely returned. On the off chance she answered, I was met with the same coldness I had come to know from my mother. I was never told what had caused the rift, but I never saw my aunt in person again after my last visit. That final trip was just before I turned eighteen and even then I felt a shift in affection for me. I'd catch her staring at me from across the room, only to look away when I noticed.

After I'd left for college, I would usually return home on the holidays or for the odd special occasion and birthday. Don't get me wrong, I loved my parents, but it was difficult not to get wrapped up in the freedom of a life on my own. College wasn't far, but it was distant enough to rule out returning home for the weekend. My visits were usually planned weeks in advance. It was only after an exceptionally rough breakup that I made an impulsive decision to visit home without first alerting my parents. At that time, The Family was the last thing on my mind.

By happenstance, that visit, heavy with emotional turmoil, coincided with The Family's annual arrival. Needless to say, my hopeful expectations for affection and comfort were not exactly met. I arrived in the afternoon, after The Family had checked in. I found my mother in the office in unusually uplifted spirits, but still distant. She greeted me with a hug and mentioned The Family in passing. Once again, the strangeness surrounding them was ignored. It didn't occur to her to question why I was there without notice; she just went about tidying up the check-in desk. I assumed it would come up at dinner, but she never did get around to asking me.

The Family kept to themselves, locked in the same room they always rented. I sometimes forgot they were even in there, hidden by the heavy black-out curtains. But they were there, the same as always, and just as I remembered them. They'd spend their days behind those fabric ramparts and would only leave at night. Even with everything on the mountain closed at those hours, they were always dressed for something special. Each of them carried a unique style as if influenced by a decade fashion had moved far beyond. The men dressed in thick cotton shirts, wool trousers, and heavy tweed jackets. The Boy looked as though he had seen all of James Dean's films and decided to adopt only his edgiest looks. The women wore dresses most would reserve for Sunday service, with the older one making a point to always accessorize with an assortment of antique jewelry. The Teenage Girl was the only one whose style would sometimes vary, but most of her dresses seemed to be sourced from a 1960s Sears catalog. The youngest, The Little Girl, seemed to wear the same few dresses over and over. Oddly enough, her clothes were the only aspect of The Family that seemed to age. It set her apart from them. The flaws in her tattered clothes read like an innocence the rest of them lacked with their immaculate outfits. My mother must have noticed because, on more than one shopping trip for school, I remember her buying an outfit that clearly wasn't for me. She would discreetly slip the gift-wrapped clothes to The Old Man upon check-out. It seemed to give her some small sense of joy, to help out this strange little girl.

On that visit, eager to distract myself from my recent heartbreak, I began helping a little more. Every evening I would clean the room after The Family left. At first, my father was wary of accepting my help, but my mother reminded him that I'd have to take over one day. For some reason, this seemed to make him sad. He tried to hide it, but it was clear he was not eager to pass on The Family business.

From then on, whenever I was home, I took on evening service. On that particular visit though, it was only The Family I cleaned up after. No other rooms had been rented.

Their beds were always made, and the room was otherwise tidy except for the ashtrays. Whoever it was—The Old

Man, I suspected—smoked like a chimney. Even after my parents stopped allowing smoking inside the motel, they made an exception for The Family. Every night, I would empty the ashtray, take out the trash, and vacuum the carpet. The mundane repetition did well to distract me from the trauma of total isolation and I grew to enjoy it. This odd sense of escape was probably why I returned home after my post-college years failed to develop into a fulfilling life. I could clean rooms anywhere, but there was something about that old motel room that helped me detach from the harsh reality of my own lonely life.

I had developed a meditative routine in cleaning, so I was a bit disappointed when my mother insisted on taking care of their room on my last night there. It was also the last night of The Family's reservation, and for reasons that were not apparent at the time, it caused my father a lot of stress. It started in the afternoon while The Family were still locked behind their blackout curtains. He paced back and forth in the lobby, mumbling to himself. He then spent over an hour doing an inventory of cleaning supplies and materials we used to patch up and repair damaged rooms. He snapped at my mother when he realized they only had one roll of wallpaper left that matched the pattern in the room.

"How was I to know they'd discontinue it?" he shouted from the other room.

My mother, on the other hand, was calm but clearly in a somber mood. She always seemed to deflate on the day before The Family checked out. Neither of my parents were themselves that day.

When my father began to brew a second pot of coffee at eleven thirty, I told him I was getting in bed.

He flashed me a distracted smile and turned his attention back to the window, watching the door to their room. Normally, they would check-out shortly after sundown, so this delay only agitated him even more.

It was well after midnight when The Family finally left, but my parents had stayed awake, waiting for their exit. While I was asleep, they wasted no time in starting the post-check-out deep clean. Most rooms, even at their worst, would take no more than an hour or two. This time, my parents were still cleaning when the car arrived the next morning to take me to the airport. They said their hurried goodbyes through a cracked door as bleach fumes and the heavy scent of rusted iron wafted out from behind them. I was in a hurry so I didn't pay much attention to it, but this was not the last time they would spend hours cleaning up after The Family departed.

Even in their later years, when I handled almost everything, my parents would still insist on cleaning The Family's room on that final day. Despite the general tidiness in the days leading to their departure, my parents would take hours to clean after The Family's exit. On one particular visit, my father had come down with a terrible cold and had little energy. Still, my mother would not let me assist. I watched for hours as they came and went from the room carrying full trash bags and empty bottles of bleach.

"What are you doing in there, scrubbing the grout with a toothbrush?" I quipped to my mother as she stepped into the office, sweaty and exhausted.

I expected a chuckle, but instead I received a tired, questioning glare. She retrieved another jug of bleach and left without so much as thank you for holding the door. Neither she nor my father returned until well after midnight. My father's cold lingered for another week, long after he should have recovered.

Shortly after I had officially moved back, but before I had a chance to settle in, The Family visited. Their stay was largely uneventful and I barely saw them due to my focus on unpacking. On the final night, I found my mother in the lobby, watching their room through the window, wet with fog. She was waiting for them to leave.

"Do you ever look at their reservation and just dread their check out?" I asked, startling her.

She turned, with a sad look in her eyes, and asked "Why would I dread it?"

"Seems like a lot of work without much appreciation for it," I replied, trying to keep it light.

"That's what being a parent is," she said, turning back to the window.

After The Family had left, my parents took nearly two days to deep clean that room, but still, they wouldn't allow me to help. Slowly, in the months after that, I took on more roles at the motel and my parents slid into semi-retirement.

After over a decade of learning the ropes, my father had finally come to terms with me taking on the family business. Still, they always insisted on cleaning up after The Family's final night.

After The Family's last visit while my parents were still alive, I had to help my father carry carpet into the room. We had spare rolls saved in my sister's old room, in case we ever had to fix a cigarette burn or a particularly nasty stain. We usually only needed a few inches or a foot at a time. The carpet in The Family's room, however, had been replaced more times than I could count. This last time, my father was tired and struggled with the work. I could tell my mother didn't want me to help, but they had no choice. They had already pulled up the old carpet before I was allowed in, but I still noticed it. Outside the bathroom, deep brown stains had soaked into the wooden floorboards beneath the padding. My mother was still scrubbing when I carried in the replacement roll.

"Is that blood?" I asked, pointing at the frothy pink foam beneath her weathered brush.

She shot my father with a look of anger.

"They are hunters," he said with a dismissive wave of his hand.

The dark-stained ring that always seemed to exist in the bathtub of this room suddenly started to make sense.

"For all the years they've stayed here, I don't actually know much about them," I admitted.

His words were curt: "Neither do we."

"I mean, this is a lot of blood..." I said, trailing off and hoping for more answers.

"It was probably a big animal," my father replied, annoyed.

"And we just let them slaughter it in our bathroom? That has to be against some sort of health code," I chuckled.

All he could muster was a shrug. "People are stuck in their ways, I guess."

It made absolutely no sense to slaughter an animal in a motel bathroom, but that was just one more absurd aspect of The Family. I wanted to push for answers, but I realized I wouldn't be getting any from my father. He was tired, and it was clear he hated the fact that I was helping with this macabre cleanup.

I let it be. I figured I'd ask again in two years, wait until their next visit.

I didn't get a chance though, as both of my parents passed within months of each other about a year after that last visit. I'd like to say they died peacefully at home, same as my sister, but they did not. My father had a heart attack, and even though he was transported to the hospital via helicopter, it was still not fast enough. He died in transit, and while they were able to revive him upon arrival, he had already lost everything that made him, him.

As we weighed the options for my father's care, the stress was too much for my mother. While still at his bedside in the hospital, she suffered a massive stroke. For a time, the two of them shared the same room full of the hauntingly familiar sounds of the machines used to delay death. Sometimes, in the quietest moments in the middle of the night, I can still hear those syncopated beeps.

Despite the doctor's best efforts, my father died for a second time shortly after my mother's stroke. He wasn't even aware of her presence six feet away from him when he passed. My mother, however, was very aware when he finally left her. She seemed to hold on for longer than anybody thought possible. Even with her husband gone, she seemed to be waiting for something. Had she wanted, she could have revealed what it was, but she never did. We closed the motel for those few awful months so that I could spend my time with both of them. My father was never really aware of my presence, and my mother, she just didn't seem to care. I'd like to say that our final moments together were spent exchanging words of love and lament with each other, but they were not. It was only a few months after my father's death that my mother died in her sleep with a look of immense sadness on her face. The next day I returned to the mountain and reopened the motel. I didn't know what else to do and for some reason, I believe it's what they would have wanted. In a weird way, I felt like I was honoring them by doing so.

At their wake, I was shaken by how few people attended their service. It wasn't that I expected old regulars to make the trip out, or the entire mountain community to show, but I did expect to see some familiar faces. I saw none. Those who arrived were either cousins I had never met or people my parents had worked with in their decades of running the motel. Though it was nice to finally put a face to the name of the woman who placed our cleaning supply orders, I felt sad that none of them shared the same grief. I had called my aunt, but she didn't answer—any of the four times I tried. For each message I left, I made sure to include the address and time of the wake, in case she decided to show.

Graham, bless his heart, had made it a point to stop by, even though he missed the viewing. I was standing out back, listening to the crickets chirp as they sang off the sunlight and welcomed in the cotton candy hues of dusk. The mountains loomed above us, and the peaks where I knew my motel stood were coated in thick white clouds. I took a sip from my father's flask and tucked it into my back pocket. I was never a big drinker, but it felt like a nice way to honor my old man. He only shared a sip with me two times: once on my twenty-first birthday and again when I finally graduated college. The etching on the side of the flask read "only for use in celebration or sorrow" and he always made a point to justify which occasion we were drinking for. He would have gotten a kick out of me using it that night. I could picture him asking in his old gravelly voice, "So which one is it, kid?"

Graham gave the slight nod-and-wave one does when you want to skip over catching up. I hadn't seen him in a couple of years, but neither of us wanted to bring the other up to speed, not under these circumstances.

The shaggy blonde hair from his youth had been cleaned up into a "respectable length" you'd expect from a government employee. His skinny frame had filled out and his thick glasses had been replaced by contacts. I chuckled at the thought of Ginny Martin seeing him now regretting saying no when he asked her to prom all those years ago. I'm fairly certain Graham never gave it a second thought, though. He was never one to dwell on the past.

"You think it looks more or less lonely from down here?" he asked, walking across the gravel parking lot.

"It's hard to imagine anybody living up there, even though I do," I chuckled.

"You're not alone," he said, looking up at the mountains.

"Thank you for making the trek out here. I know it's a drive, so really, thank you. I was hoping to see your parents too, though."

"Well, as I said, you're not alone up there. I moved back a week or so ago. Took a leave. My ma and pa aren't doing so hot, so I decided to come down here in their place," he said, his throat catching at the mention of his mother. I could tell it hurt him.

"I'm sorry to hear that." I offered him a nip from my flask. Suddenly, it felt like high school all over again. He took it.

"Yup," he said with a heavy sigh.

"How long do you suppose you're here for?" I asked, then immediately regretted the implications.

"I mean, I guess it depends. I put in for a transfer, so it could be a while. But you know, if that doesn't happen before they..." he shrugged, inferring the rest.

"Well, feel free to stop by for coffee any time. I know you're probably busy, but if you need any, you know, *you time,* I'll be around to chat."

"How long do you suppose for?" he asked, laughing a little.

"Good question," I replied.

As was expected, my parents left the motel to me. The lawyer explained that their will was brief and uncomplicated. After their medical expenses, my parents had no money saved in the bank and since the motel was their only asset, I was given everything. Debt, clutter, and a future of isolation were my only inheritance.

In addition to the burden of our family business, I was left with instructions on how to manage it. Three very old envelopes written many years before, the paper yellowed with age, were handed to me by the lawyer. Each one had specific instructions on when to open them.

—The first was to be opened when I took ownership of the motel.

—The second was to be opened only in case of an emergency—namely a financial one.

—The third was to be opened by my aunt in the event I passed away before she did.

The letter inside the first envelope was brief and to the point. It explained that my parents had a long-standing agreement with The Family and it was best not to question it.

The bloodstains on the floor were mentioned, but they were adamant that I not ask questions. I was instructed to "just clean it up" and to make sure there was no trace of The Family left once they checked out. It was very explicit that I didn't question The Family. Additionally, if anybody outside of The Family were to ask about them, I was to deny everything. There was also a vague mention of "consequences greater than death," but it looked as if it were added as an afterthought—a weird threatening addendum in an already strange letter. It ended with mundane instructions on how to settle their bill and log their reservation. It was simple, which only made the directions preceding it even stranger.

In something I found funny and not surprising, The Family's odd trait of never aging wasn't mentioned in the letter. After reading through it twice, I stashed it along with the two unopened letters in the cash drawer and forgot about them.

I had only closed the motel for a few days to handle the affairs, but by the time I returned, there was already a booking. I felt my eyelid twitch with anxiety at the realization that I was totally on my own from there on out. The fact that nobody had responded to my "help wanted" ad only deepened my feelings of isolation. That being said, I was happy to have something to distract me; furthermore, it was a familiar name on the reservation. With the caves closed for refurbishment, I wasn't expecting many guests and I was dreading the loneliness. Seeing the name G. Edward Ballard was a welcome surprise.

I should mention that while the motel was located near a tourist spot, there was little else to attract people. Better gas mileage and the lure of more familiar corporate hotel chains were just two of the factors that eroded our business. We were small and out of the way for most people. It was rare for anyone to stop and stay the night unless they planned for it ahead of time. The days of driving until you had to sleep were long gone and with it, a large part of our traffic. If not for the caves, that would have been the nail in the coffin, but my parents somehow persisted for years on the ever-dwindling tourist money.

It didn't help that we were located on what they called a dead road, a long stretch of highway without any signs of civilization. These were the highways where people seemed to go missing. Sometimes the victims were found just a bit off the road, but more often than not, it was the last place they were seen. We'd had our fair share of mysterious travelers that seemed to disappear after staying with us. The next of kin would call, and questions would be asked, but it was rare they found what they were looking for. It was even more rare if they found *who* they were looking for.

One case in particular that always stuck with me, happened while I was in high school. The disappearance of a twenty-year-old woman named Peach Summers. The implied innocence of her name was already enough to make headlines. That, coupled with the strange circumstances surrounding the discovery of her body, made national headlines for a brief news cycle.

Peach had left her home in the middle of the night. Her parents discovered her and the family car missing in the morning when her father left for work. Peach was working on her cosmetology license and had taken a job helping the elderly at a retirement home to pay for it. Her manager reported that she unexpectedly quit on the day before her disappearance. Her parents were unaware of this at the time. Her body was discovered eight weeks later near the Bloodridge Caverns National Park.

Nobody is quite sure why she left or where she was headed, but confirmed signings of her journey surfaced shortly after the discovery of her body. At the request of her parents and the police, a photo of her was plastered across television screens and newspapers, begging for any information on what she may have been doing in the weeks between her disappearance and death. She had been seen at gas stations and motels across the country at seemingly random intervals. The last reported sighting came from my father, who had checked her into our motel two weeks before her body was found by a park ranger.

I was there the day she checked in. Her eyes darted back and forth behind the thin whisps of stringy hair that hung in her face. Dark circles framed her bloodshot eyes, black with dilation. As she spoke, she would pause between words to gnaw at her fingernails, or rather, the place where her fingernails should have been. Instead, she had raw scabby stumps where her nails had been pulled off. The way she nervously chewed on her thumb made me believe it was her own doing. She looked so different from the pictures they showed on the television, that neither I nor my father realized it was her. It was only after the authorities showed up to question us that the connection was made.

Her car was found on a private road that splintered off the main highway. The discovery of her car led to the discovery of her body.

She was found half buried in the dirt with her throat slit and a mouth full of soil. From the evidence they collected, including the dirt beneath her fingernails and the single set of footprints, it appeared that she may have buried herself. But that seemed unlikely given the traumatic injuries. I remember my father being strangely defensive in his answers, declining to let the investigators explore our property, though he did show them the room she stayed in. I overheard him speaking to my mother, expressing concern that they would return, but they never did.

Our dead road and Peach's case in particular is what brought G. Edward Ballard into my life. He strolled in with a small-town demeanor and an expensive leather side bag. The buttons were left open at his collar and his sleeves were rolled past his elbow. He looked as though he was perpetually working overtime but didn't seem to mind it.

"That's a fancy name, what does the G. stand for?" I asked the first time he checked in.

"Gary."

I pointed over to a portrait of my father with his father. "Gary was my grandfather's name. Why the initial?"

"Because Gary Ballard sounds like I sell steak knives or life insurance."

"Yeah, well, G. Edward Ballard sounds like a writer," I laughed.

He looked embarrassed, scratching at his five o'clock shadow. "Well... actually," he chuckled.

"No kidding? What do you write?"

"True crime." He smiled.

We quickly bonded over our shared interest in reading. This was back when my parents were still active around the motel, so I had a bit of free time to chat and hang out and read. G. Edward Ballard, or as I called him, Gary, spent a lot of time in our lobby by the fire. We offered free wifi, but the signal was iffy more than fifty feet from the front desk. Gary and I often found ourselves surfing the web from the comfort of the large red velvet couch that faced the fireplace. Oftentimes we would chat over coffee, and he would share new evidence for whatever book he was working on. The reason for his visit, and all future returns, was the same: research for a book. It was about what he called "The Ring of Fire," a connection of dead roads all across the country.

"A giant asphalt ring of paved death," he said with a grin.

He explained that a lot of famous serial killers traveled the ring; some I'd heard of, but most I hadn't. His book was going to connect the dots between unclaimed victims and known routes of the killers.

"Are there a lot of them? Serial killers?" I asked.

"More than you'd think. In fact, odds are you've met at least one in your lifetime. Probably even here." He smirked, leaning back on the sofa.

This fact would stick with me for years, even though he told me that I shouldn't worry about it.

He quickly tried to walk it back. "You're safe. The dead are always faceless. It's always sex workers, or indigenous folk, or just some drifters who lost their way."

"That's terrible."

"The real tragedy is that they get a lot less attention. They are considered less dead to the cops. Their deaths don't mean as much as a politician or a pretty white girl."

"Like Peach Summers?" I asked.

"Like Peach Summers," he nodded.

Despite the morbid nature of his visits, I still looked forward to catching up on the progress of his book. That particular visit, maybe more so than ever.

Almost immediately, I noticed a change in him. He looked a little more road-worn and weary. The charming sparkle in his pale blue eyes had gone and he wore the heavy dark rings of restless sleep.

With just the two of us at the motel, I offered to make dinner. I'd never really cooked for anyone other than my parents, but I was hungry for the company. Gary checked in and unpacked, then went to the lobby to finish up some emails and other affairs while I cooked.

When he finally joined me in the kitchen, he was quiet and unusually distant. In the past, I'd fight to get a word in as he babbled on about all the news he had for me. This time, I could barely get a full sentence from him.

Across the table, I watched as he cut into the steak my father had frozen in hopes of cooking it on his birthday. My dad liked Gary, so I felt like it was appropriate.

He finally spoke in between a particularly large bite, "This is very good. Thank you."

"I'm glad. Thank you for having dinner with me. When I saw your name, I got a little excited to have some familiar company. It's been, what, a little over a year now?"

He cut into another piece. "Just shy of it."

I waited for him to follow that up with something, but instead, he took another bite.

"So, how's the book?" I asked with genuine interest.

"It's... umm..." He put down the fork and knife. "It's falling apart actually. Every time I learn something new, the less I seem to understand. The threads don't connect anymore. And my publisher doesn't believe me. Or in me, I guess."

"I'm sorry to hear that, but I know what you mean."

He sat back with a smile, finally relaxing a little. "I told him I think The Ring of Fire Killer might be only one person. You know, rather than many, and I think they've been operating for well over sixty years at this point."

"No kidding? What about the file cabinet of suspects you had?"

"I found something. It doesn't make any sense though."

"Less sense than a geriatric ax murderer?" I laughed.

"I think it's a ritual thing. Satanic maybe? Or just psychotic. I don't know, but... let me ask you this: what is something you believe in, but keep it to yourself because it... just sounds too crazy?"

"You mean like god or aliens?"

"I'm serious, what do you keep to yourself because it's too out there?"

I shifted nervously in my chair. I knew Gary, but I didn't know him *that* well.

Noticing my discomfort, he spoke again. "Okay, I'll go first. I think that satanic ritual abuse actually happens and there is some truth to the whole endocrine-eating elite stuff."

A normal, polite response escaped me. "So, you're a conspiracy nut now?"

"No!" he objected. "Okay, well, I mean, other than this one. I just think there is some strange shit out there. Evil is real; I've seen it, and maybe it's got a hunger for...glands." He chuckled at his own words, acknowledging how absurd it sounded.

"Alright... You're right; it does make you sound crazy. But just a little bit," I laughed, tossing my head back, enjoying the moment of genuine human connection. I hadn't realized how much I missed being around regular people.

"Okay, your turn," he prodded.

My mind went immediately to The Family. He must have noticed because he leaned forward. "You've got something good, don't you?"

I thought of the letter and the instructions that my parents had left me. I thought of the dire warning written in my mother's handwriting. I thought about all the years that The Family had checked into my life and how no matter how long it had been, they always looked the same. I thought of the blood and the strange hours they kept. I thought about how the next time they checked in, I would be by myself. I thought about how my parents had kept this secret until the day they died and even then they didn't bother to explain it. I thought about the fact that it was just one more burden they had placed on me upon their death. And then I thought, what harm could it really do if I told him?

Gary was my friend, and if I was going to tell anybody about the ageless guests that check in every two years, he would be the last person to call me crazy. So, I told him everything I could remember about this odd family that never seemed to age. I told him about the older couple, the middle aged man and woman, the two teenagers, and the young girl. I told him about their old car, their odd hours, and the strange way they dressed. I told him everything— well, almost everything.

I left out the part about the blood-stained carpet, purely for the sake of not incriminating myself.

Thinking back, that was probably the one thing I shouldn't have kept from him.

My mother had been gone a little over a month when The Family arrived. There had been a handful of overnight guests since Gary had checked out, but not enough to free me from the overwhelming sense of solitude. Regardless of the strange circumstances surrounding them, I was looking forward to seeing The Family's all-too-familiar faces again. I was craving any kind of human interaction.

The sun had long gone down when the seven pale figures piled out of their familiar old station wagon and walked together into my office. I greeted them with a cheerful wave.

"Hello," said The Old Man, buttoning up his dusty tweed jacket. His tone was oddly indifferent, neither friendly nor hostile. It felt practiced but forced, like he was reading from a script he memorized a long time ago.

Without my parents there to insist on doing it themselves, this was the first time I had checked The Family in. The Old Man proceeded to discuss the details of their stay as if he knew me.

"We will only be staying a few nights. We will give notice on our final day. Until then, we request service only after we depart for the evening."

I smiled and nodded. "Of course."

In the same expressionless tone, he asked, "Do you have any matches?"

"Not at the desk, but I'll go grab you some," I said, remembering the box my father had ordered for The Old Man just before he passed. It was still wrapped up with some other fresh supplies on the kitchen counter.

"Please, do," he said, with a strangely demanding air.

I guess I expected some acknowledgment that, until that moment, we'd never actually spoken. If he were a new guest, it wouldn't have been odd. Considering the relationship he had with my parents, though, I expected him to at least recognize that I was their child, but if he did, I'd never know.

He didn't ask about my parents, and in a weird, indescribable way, he spoke to me as if I had always been the one to check them in.

"I appreciate your continued efforts to accommodate us," he said, taking the small matchbook I retrieved from the box in the kitchen.

"Of course," I replied.

His tone was robotic: "Thank you again for your understanding of our needs. We will be staying in this evening. No need for a turndown."

All but The Little Girl seemed to watch me, dead-eyed and without expression. Instead, she broke away from the group and stepped around the desk to knock on the door leading to our kitchen. None of The Family reacted to her intrusive actions.

"Can I help you?" I asked, momentarily stunned by her sudden change in behavior. There was tenderness to her curiosity, a vulnerability the others in her family lacked.

She cocked her head to the side, confused. "Isn't she in there?"

"My mom? It's just me now. My parents passed away a few months back." I explained as I grabbed the room key.

The older man took it without so much as a hint of recognition that my parents were dead. The Little Girl though, she broke down sobbing. She called for her mother between snotty gasping breaths. Neither The Middle Aged Woman nor The Old Woman seemed to notice. I felt bad for her.

Instead, The Teenage Girl took the little one by the arm and pulled her along as they left. The child's sad eyes met mine and for a moment I felt an unspoken grief between us over my parents' absence. I realized it was the first time that anybody outside of myself had shown any anguish over their loss. It felt... good. It made me feel less alone in this isolated little motel. I watched as The Family dragged

The Little Girl by her arm, back to their room to unpack and settle in.

As The Teenage Boy and The Middle Aged Man unloaded a large steamer trunk from the car, they watched The Little Girl cry with an odd sense of confusion. Her emotions almost seemed foreign to them. This made me feel even worse for the misunderstood young child. It was the first time I felt a sort of kinship with The Little Girl. The two of us were isolated by circumstances beyond our control. We had an unspoken bond of loneliness. Before that, I always just saw her as one of them.

I thought back to their last few visits and remembered how my mother used to treat this little girl. She must have seen the same thing I did. My mother always seemed to dote on her and pay special attention to her needs. After my sister's death, my mother was less than affectionate, even to me. Still, she seemed to make time for this little girl who only came around every two years. I can only assume my mother saw my sister in her. My heart hurt for the both of us.

Later that evening, I passed their room during my nightly routine. I heard the whip-crack sounds of an old western gunfight on their television, which had been turned up to maximum volume. Luckily, there were no other guests to complain about it. I was going to let it be, but a loud crash from inside the room drew me back to their door. Standing outside, I heard a dreadful low moan that was almost buried by the audio of a saloon fight. Long, pained howls came from somewhere deep in the room, muffled as if guarded by another door inside, a room within the room.

I knocked, but there was no answer. The guttural whine of a creature in pain echoed beneath the tinny, canned piano music playing out of the television speakers.

I knocked again.

The haunting moan broke into choking sobs, and I could feel the visceral sorrow of the thing that produced them. No living creature could produce the unholy sounds coming from inside that room. Still, I thought immediately of The Little Girl.

Worried, I knocked one last time.

In a single moment, the television was silenced, and the pained cries ceased with it. The light behind the heavy curtains went out. I convinced myself that the strange sound that I heard had been part of the show they were watching. As unlikely as it seemed, I decided it was in my best interest to believe it.

The Family did not leave their room that night, but I assumed that was because they couldn't. They had nowhere to go. I later found out that a car accident halfway down the mountain had stopped all traffic. A car had swerved and hit a tree, which in turn brought the old rotted pine down on the highway. The driver was gravely injured. They knew this because of the massive amounts of smeared blood left on the steering wheel, even though the body wasn't found. It was assumed the driver had wandered into the woods after suffering a head injury and from there fell prey to the untamed forestland that stretched for miles. Most likely consumed by the wildlife that stalked the mountain.

The car itself wasn't found until a highway patrolman came upon it. There were no witnesses, so they weren't sure when the crash happened. I did find it curious that even the broadest guess put the time of the accident hours before The Family arrived. How they had made it up the mountain past the tree and wreckage was anybody's guess.

Their stay was uneventful, and after that night, even The Little Girl all but ignored my presence. With the accident cleaned up, they managed to go out a few times over the next few nights, always returning before morning and always without notice. Until their last night, the room again was tidy except for the cigarettes. The source of the loud crash I heard on the first night remained a mystery.

As they loaded their car on their final night, I decided to re-read the letter from the first envelope one more time. I went over the checkout instructions like I was double-checking a shopping list. For their reservation, I was given a list of fake names and told to rotate through them when penciling in The Family's next stay. I was told specifically not to ask for their real names. Unsurprisingly, the next two future visits were already entered into the system by my father. Everything after was left blank. I guess it was his way of letting me take the reins. The letter also noted that they would pay in cash and leave behind a small paper package, sealed with twine. I was instructed to never open the parcel, but instead, put it in a safe. A safe, I should add,

I had no idea existed before reading the letter. It was located beneath the floorboards in my parent's room in what I always thought was a crawl space. Using the combination left for me, I did as the letter instructed. Inside the safe, I found more small paper bundles tied with twine. I placed the new one with the others and moved on to the next part of the letter. I'd be lying if I said I couldn't feel the threads of curiosity pulling at the back of my mind, but I did what I'd always been taught: I moved on without question.

The thing is, what I found cleaning their room on that final night made it difficult to ignore. There was the brief mention in the note and the dry stains on the ripped-up carpet, but I'd dealt with that before. In all those years though, I'd only ever seen the aftermath. There was nothing in the note that hinted at the reality of it. There was nothing to prepare me for the amount of blood The Family left behind.

It was no crime scene, but it was more than a few blotches and spatters that could be wiped away with a wet paper towel. Even though bleaching the floors had already become a normal step in our cleaning process, this required much more than the usual amount.

I'd seen the aftermath of a bloody nose or an accidental artery nick. This was not that. The real cause for concern was the evidence of blood rather than blood itself. The bathtub had clearly been filled with it and then drained, leaving behind a red-brown ring of film. The tiled floors were sticky where there had been an attempt to wipe it up, and the carpet had soaked up whatever had bled out of the bathroom.

The task seemed monumental, but I had done my best to mentally prepare for it. I replaced the carpet as my father had shown me and scrubbed the bathroom until there was no trace left. I ended up using a full bottle of bleach and could no longer smell anything beyond the potent chemical odor of the cleaning products.

Looking back, of course it seemed suspicious, but it was always that way with The Family. My parents always made a point of mentioning The Family's peculiar interest in hunting. It's important to note, I didn't recall ever seeing them unpack a bow, gun, or weapon of any sort from their old station wagon. Just their normal luggage and that large steamer trunk, the contents of which were still a mystery. Reasonably, I couldn't say for sure where the blood came from, but I never wanted to ask. Had anybody come around with questions, like the cops, I'd like to think I would have said something. But in all those years, nobody ever did.

I continued to tell myself that there was nothing to worry about. They were nothing more than a normal family on their annual hunting trip. Sure, they happened to be dressed in fashions that spanned the decades, but who was I to judge? Fashion was never my thing, and honestly, neither was family bonding. It certainly took effort to accept them as big game enthusiasts, considering I'd never seen them with a firearm. And even though sometimes at night, their eyes shone black like a shark's, it was still easier to accept them as a family of odd hobbyists than a family of serial killers. Honestly, I was just doing what I had always done. What my parents had always done. I accepted their lies without question because it made my life just a little bit easier.

Every so often, The Family would accidentally leave something behind. Usually, I'd store it in my sister's old room for a couple of years and then leave it on their bed the next time they checked in. Sometimes it was a sock or the odd piece of jewelry, but mostly it was old books and magazines. If they didn't want it, they'd move it to the small bathroom trash can.

On one occasion it was an innocuous empty matchbook sitting next to the mountain of cigarette butts that overflowed from the ashtray. I'm not entirely sure why it caught my attention. Maybe it was because matchbooks, unlike other disposable trinkets, carry a story with them. They have a past. Sometimes they tell you where the holder has been. This matchbook did just that. The name of the establishment, "Ocean Point Inn," was printed in gold embossed lettering. On the back, beneath the address, was a phone number. Curiosity crept in like a chill through an open flue.

I knew so little about The Family and part of me wanted to keep it that way, but the other part, well, it won out. If I was going to be cleaning up their mess for the rest of my life, maybe I should find out how other people dealt with it.

I rang the number printed on the back.

"Hi, I'm calling to inquire about some guests that may have stayed with you recently. I own an overnight establishment myself and I..." I struggled to come up with a believable lie. "I don't have the right number or contact. But they left something very important here and I'd like to get it back to them."

The voice on the other line was leery of my rambling inquiry, "Okay... Do you have a name?"

"I don't. They pay in cash, but it's a family. Seven of them. Two men, two women, a boy, and two girls. They drive an older model..."

"Okay. Yeah," they interrupted.

"Yeah, you know them?"

"I know who you're talking about," the voice over the phone confirmed.

"Great. Do you think I can get their contact info?"

"I'm sorry. That's not possible. You understand."

"Okay, well, let me ask you this," I tried to pivot. "This might be weird, but have they stayed with you before?"

There was a long pause on the other end before strikingly hesitant, "Yeah."

"Okay, this is even weirder. How long have you worked there? More than a couple years?"

Another long pause.

"Who are you again?" they asked.

"I work at an establishment that they frequent. It's funny, for some reason we don't have a contact number or anything, really."

I waited for a response, but all I heard was the sound of heavy breathing.

"I...I found your matchbook. They left it behind."

There was another pause, but this time I could hear a hand muffle the receiver. They had what sounded like a tense exchange with another person in the room. Then, the other person was on the line. A woman with a rough, weathered voice croaked out a warning. "If you have to ask, you aren't ready for the answers. They will destroy you."

"Are you talking about The Family or the answers?" I asked, a weak attempt at a joke.

She didn't appreciate my humor and, after a moment of silent judgment, she croaked, "You should know the rules. If you've made an agreement, you should know the rules. We can't help you."

"What agreement?" I asked.

A tiny bit of sympathy crept into her scratchy, worn-out voice. "May God help you then."

The line went dead. I dialed again, but there was no answer. I tried again a few days later, but neither of the people

I had spoken with ever answered again. I tucked the match-book into a drawer and eventually forgot about it. Every so often, her words would creep into the back of my mind, but with nowhere else to go, I would forget again. I considered the idea of asking The Family, maybe inquiring about the agreement they had with my parents. But that would have meant broaching the subject and acknowledging some of the more *questionable services* we provided. The subject of the cleanup alone would open a whole other can of worms I wasn't sure I wanted to deal with. Confrontation had never been my strong suit. If anybody truly wanted me to know about any of this, I felt they would have told me, whether my parents or The Family. Their secrecy was unsettling and it felt like uncovering it would lead to things I wasn't ready to deal with. I decided my parents probably withheld certain things for the sake of my safety, which made the idea of asking The Family particularly unpleasant. I wres-tled with this for a very long time, the safety of ignorance versus the power of knowledge.

I ended up sticking with ignorance. It was going to be a long time before The Family returned and there was no point in dwelling. Honestly, I probably would've forgotten about the Ocean Point Inn entirely if another one of their matchbooks hadn't come across my check-in desk.

It was maybe a year or so after the last visit from The Family and I hadn't thought about the matchbook or the inn for months. Things had slowed down a bit and my mind was consumed with ways to breathe life back into my failing family business.

Walk-in bookings weren't completely unheard of, but when the park shut down, they became extremely rare. The night Herman Dalin, an older gentleman with a sloped nose and narrow jaw, walked through the door, the rain was coming down in sheets so thick that I didn't see his headlights pull into the parking lot.

I was sitting at the front desk with a hot mug of tea and a magazine that was so old that it felt new again. He stepped inside, quickly shut the door behind him, dried off, and stowed his umbrella in the bucket by the door. I nodded a polite hello and smiled. He smiled back but waited until he reached the desk to speak.

"Good evening. Do you offer long-term rentals?" he asked in a kind and reassuring voice.

"Not normally, no, but I suppose we can arrange it. How long are we talking? Weeks? A month?" I asked, opening the calendar.

Herman dug into his pockets, looking for something. As he spoke, he placed various items on the counter, "I'm not too sure," he said, setting down his keys. "I'm actually waiting for someone." His wallet came next. "I just want to make sure this is a place where I can wait for them. The last place I was staying had a limit. Asked me to leave," he said, nodding to the Ocean Point Inn matchbook as he placed it on the counter. My eyes must have lingered on that match-book for a moment too long because he cleared his voice and asked, "You know them?"

"Can't say I do, and I've never heard of that policy, personally. As long as you pay, you can stay," I laughed, trying to ignore the matchbook.

He smiled, paid, and gathered up his things, matchbook included. He paused for a moment, holding the matches between his thumb and forefinger before tapping them on the counter.

"Do you happen to have any of these?" he asked.

"With our name? No, not since we stopped offering smoking rooms," I lied, knowing full well a small box of matches was still under the desk in case one particular guest asked for them. I don't know why I lied about it, such a harmless thing, but there was just something I didn't trust about the Ocean Point Inn and, by association, him.

However, with business as quiet as it was, there was no way I was turning down the much-needed income, and I was happy to have company.

Herman paid upfront for the week and, after that, we decided to settle up every other day. My initial distrust faded over time as I got to know him better. Every so often, I'd ask him how long he was planning to stay or, rather, wait, but his answer was always the same: a shrug.

Herman remained in his room most of the time, watching television or reading. He would leave to take walks around the grounds, but usually stuck close to the highway and was never gone more than a half hour. The longest he would leave would be when he'd drive down the hill for groceries. We didn't usually allow hot plates, but I wasn't in a position to care. He was keeping me afloat while other travelers trickled in, slower than usual. I also let him use his small barbeque in the parking lot, and we moved a mini fridge in after the first week. Our ice maker couldn't keep up with his cooler of groceries. He cooked regularly from what I could tell, but he always kept to himself. If he had any guests, I never saw them.

Occasionally, Herman would order a pizza from the shop a little way down the mountain. After the first time they showed up to deliver, I told the driver to always add a cheese and garlic for me. I felt bad for them making the trek and I wanted to make it worth their while. The last thing you want to do when living in a remote location is to piss off the only pizza place for miles. A single order of eggrolls lost us delivery privileges from my father's favorite restaurant, and he had checked out that guest with gritted teeth.

One day, while I was dropping off toiletries and taking out Herman's trash, I saw the now-empty matchbook in the bin. Herman was watching the weather channel. Since the coverage rarely pivoted away from rain in those months, I decided it was okay to broach the subject and interrupt his viewing.

"So, you stayed at the Ocean Point Inn?" I asked.

His attention broke from the forecast, and he looked over at me to smile and nod. "For a bit," he said.

"What kind of place is it? You're not the first guest we've had that came from there, so I was just wondering what the connection was," I asked, dumping out the trash.

It was clear my question stirred something inside of him because he wasn't quick to answer. He thought about it for a bit, as if he were trying to figure out if I meant something more.

Finally, he replied, "No connection that I know of. Similar places attracting similar clientele, I suppose."

"How far is the drive?" I asked, having only a vague idea where it was.

"A couple days, give or take. It's on the coast after all, so it depends on how direct the route is."

I wasn't content with his answer, but I didn't know what else to ask. I wanted to know more about the people who ran it, the people I'd spoken with. I began to wonder if Herman was somehow connected to The Family. My mind churned, trying to piece it together, and I guess he could tell.

"Now that I think of it, I got both of your businesses from an old travel guide of mine. The McArthur Field Guide to Road Exploration. It's pretty much an antique now, and honestly, you two are probably the last two businesses listed that are still operating," he said, satisfied that he had answered my burning question.

He turned his attention back to the television, but I prodded, "Do you have it? I'd love to see what they wrote about our little place."

Without looking he replied, "Actually, I believe I left it at Ocean Point. Sorry." And with that, our conversation ended. It may have been the longest one we had, outside of motel business.

Herman rented that room for almost four months, and I assume he would have rented it longer, had he not had the unfortunate luck to die in his sleep.

I found him on a Tuesday morning, trying to bring him fresh towels. He had passed sometime in the night, still in his clothes with the television on and a bag of chips at his side. From what I'd gathered of his habits over the past few months, I believe he died watching *Twilight Zone* reruns that would always air after midnight. I guess he could only wait for so long. It seemed age had finally taken him, which, I guess, is the best we can all hope for, really.

I contacted the authorities, and after some time, the coroner came to remove the body. Herman's wallet was on the nightstand, so I was able to find the phone number of his daughter. Along with a few others, her information was written on a clean piece of yellow-lined paper and tucked into his billfold. Behind the list of numbers was something else, carefully folded into a neat little square. It was a tattered old wedding announcement; the paper was aged and brittle to the touch. As I unfolded it, the well-worn creases came apart at the seams, but most of it was still legible. The announcement had been folded in such a way as to leave the photo of the young couple fully intact. The ink was a bit faded, but when I looked closely, my heart skipped a beat. Standing next to a young, bearded Herman was none other than The Middle Aged Woman from The Family, albeit a few years younger than I'd ever seen her. Unfortunately, her name was a casualty of disintegration.

I knew immediately that this was the woman Herman was waiting for, but I wasn't sure if this was the mother of his child. Regardless, it wasn't something I brought up when I called Herman's daughter.

When I got a hold of her, she was very sweet. She reacted as if she had been waiting for the call.

"So, where is he?" she asked with a sad quiver in her voice.

"Well, they took him down the mountain this morning. You can probably contact the morgue."

"Where's that?"

"Becket."

"I mean, what state?" she asked, her voice cracking.

It was clear she had lost track of her father, and they probably hadn't talked since before he arrived at the motel. I felt bad. Strained parental relationships were an all too familiar form of sadness.

It took her a little over a week to make arrangements and to come gather his belongings. His body was flown back to California, where she lived. He'd had enough items of value in the room and his car that it warranted her making the drive up the mountain, which she did a few days after his funeral.

This gave me enough time to clean the room and make it presentable for her. We weren't exactly bursting at the seams with reservations, so I kept his belongings in the room, right where he had left them. I did move the hot plate and fridge, though. I wasn't sure how much she knew about his plans, and I'd always been taught to respect a client's privacy. Personally, I don't find anything wrong with living in a motel, but some people judge. I didn't want him to be judged.

When she arrived, there was something striking about her. Though I knew I'd never met her before, it was clear that her mother was indeed the bride from the wedding announcement. She looked a few years older than The Middle Aged Woman from The Family, but the resemblance was undeniable. The only difference was the warmth I felt from her, something I'd never seen from her mother.

She was kind enough to book two nights even though she was only staying one.

"The second night was for the troubles and a thank you for keeping my father's things safe," she explained with a sad smile.

That evening I ordered pizza for the both of us and offered to help her pack his belongings. There was just enough to fill her trunk. She had already planned to sell his car locally and scheduled it to be picked up a few days after she left.

Over pizza, she asked me what he was like in his final days. It had been a few years since she had spent any quality time with him, so he had already become something of a ghost to her. I told her that Herman was polite and kind. I recalled a story of how he fixed a leaky faucet for me without asking. He saved me from a pricey "up the mountain" charge from the plumber.

She seemed to enjoy hearing that his last few days were peaceful.

At one point we opened a bottle of wine–her idea–and after a few glasses, I felt comfortable enough to ask questions of my own.

I poured the last of the bottle into her glass and gently broached the subject. "Do you mind if I ask who he was waiting for?"

She didn't seem to mind my question, "My mother, I think."

I felt the hairs on the back of my neck stand up.

She took a sip from her glass, and I watched as she unpacked it all in her head. "She walked out on us when I was little."

"I'm sorry to hear that," I offered.

Her eyes drifted and she began to speak like she had been waiting to tell the story. The words came pouring out as if the floodgates of her memory were opened by empathy. "She was a waitress at this old diner. The kind of place that still lets you smoke inside long after they changed the laws. Honestly, the place was older than dirt, with red vinyl seats and everything. Some of the customers had been eating there since it opened, coming in every week like clockwork. It was famous, not for the food, but for the history. It's the kind of place that gets so old that rumors of hauntings appear, like ghosts themselves. One night, after working a double, my mother came home frantic and hysterical. She was strangely combative with my father, nothing like I'd ever seen before. From my room, all I could hear was shouting between her and my father. He was trying to calm her, but that only sent her into a rage. The sound of broken glass drew me out of the safety of my room. I saw her for the last time, standing in the living room covered in mud and bleeding from her ears. The last words she ever uttered to me were an apology. Not for leaving, but for having brought me into this life in the first place," she said, drawing in a deep breath on her final word.

Her heartbreak was evident, but my curiosity got the better of me. "Where did she go?" I asked.

"We don't know. I don't even know what happened to her that night." She shook her head, lost in the memory.

I should have respected the fact that she was still in mourning, but I didn't. I couldn't help but press her for answers. The last time I had the opportunity to find out more, I held back to be polite. I wasn't going to make that mistake again.

"So, why was he waiting for her here, of all places?" I asked, curious to find the connection that Herman had previously shut down when we chatted.

Already past the point of no return, she said, "Well, she called once or twice after she left, but every time she sounded more disconnected. I think my father figured out that she had joined some sort of cult, but he never told me much. Something must have finally clicked because a few years back he sold his house and took to the road. He told me he wanted to see the country. I believed him the first go-round, but the man never stopped driving and he rarely visited me. I realized he was searching for something rather than just traveling. He never admitted it though, not to me anyhow."

I wanted to tell her that she was right, but I was afraid of saying too much. It was clear that she didn't know what had happened to her mother, what she had become. If Herman never told her, it certainly wasn't my place to try.

That night I put her in a nice clean room, far from the one her father had passed in. The next morning, I met her at the door with coffee. Once we were inside Herman's old room, I stood back and let her dictate what she wanted to tackle. Most of it she planned to pack up and deal with once she got home, like his clothing, watch, and other accessories. There were just a few boxes that she felt the need to go through before placing them in her car.

In his closet next to an old and tattered navy trunk was a normal, boring cardboard banker's box. The corner of the lid had long ago ripped, so it sat uselessly unsecured on top. Inside we found an ornate wooden box and in it was a pistol. I could tell she didn't expect it by the way she recoiled the moment her brain processed what it was. The gun sat neatly in a velvet-covered impression that fit it perfectly. Below it, nestled in their own little pockets, were a dozen polished bullets.

"Sorry, I didn't know he had this. He was never really a weapons kind of guy," she said, as if apologizing for finding it.

The next thing she found shot a hole through her previous statement. Beneath the wooden box containing the gun, she found an eight-inch dagger in a rough, rune-covered sheath. The blade was polished, same as the bullets, smooth enough to reflect her confused expression. The hilt appeared to be the jawbone of a large animal, possibly a bear or a wolf, tightly bound in sinew for grip. The sheath was made from two pieces of stitched-together rawhide, with the runes, or whatever they were, branded on it.

My fingers touched the cold steel of the blade, and I could feel the hairs on the back of my neck stand on edge. A dull numbness radiated from the blade and up my fingers. I looked up to see two uneasy eyes staring back at me, her face pale, ghost-like. I could tell she sensed the same inexplicably strange aura surrounding it. We both struggled to process what was in front of us. The cold breath of the knife crept in deeper, penetrating my bones. Everything felt wrong, but I couldn't pull away. I tried, but I couldn't. It wasn't until I felt a touch on my arm, warmth radiating from her fingers, that I was able to pull away.

"Are you okay?" she asked, reaching for my hand, clutching it tightly.

"Uh, yeah. Not really," I said, pushing the blade back into its sheath.

"What the hell is it?" she mumbled, blinking as if she were trying to clear a burned image from her eyes.

"It's a knife. I think."

"Well, it's not going in my kitchen," she said, breaking the tension. She clearly wanted to move on from whatever it was we both felt.

I pushed the strange knife away from me, putting distance between myself and its unwelcome pull. Despite the unexpected nature, or maybe because of it, I was intrigued by what else could be hidden in this cardboard box of mysteries.

Beneath a stack of clippings and collected headlines from seemingly random newspapers, there were two more items: a leather-bound book and an oddly shaped bottle of murky water. Inside the bottle, the brown sediment floated within the tinted liquid, and at the bottom, there was a thin layer of dark black soot. There had once been a label, but it had peeled off long ago, so the contents would forever remain a mystery. After the knife, neither of us dared to open it.

As strange as the other items were, the book was truly the oddest. What once began as a leather-bound tome from the turn of the century had evolved. It became a Frankenstein publication of collected notes and pages from a dozen other works. Illustrations of unusual creatures and hand-scrawled notes in unknown languages crowded the margins. Most of the words were English, but even so, the writing seemed to be at times incomprehensible. When she handed me the book, I noticed there were loose pages near the center. I opened to them, expecting to find they had come unglued. Instead, I found another booklet pressed inside so tight that it looked like it belonged there. I immediately recognized the title, "The McArthur Field Guide to Road Exploration."

It was as if Herman had kept his place with it. The pages he had marked were no more enlightening than any of the other strange occult topics contained within. Between the handwritten verses and the strange subject matter, the only thing I was able to decipher was one word, "Immortals," and even that was scribbled over in a way that conveyed frustration.

She had so many questions, and even though I had some answers, I wasn't ready to explain everything. The box appeared to be the treasured collection of a madman, but I didn't want her to remember Herman that way.

To distract her from the chilling messages scrawled in the scrap-booked grimoire, I told her about how her father said he found us by using the old guide. She got a kick out of that little tidbit about his travel life. She pulled out the flattened guide and put aside the strange book. She smiled as she leafed through it. Sure enough, we found the entry for our motel with a black and white photograph of the front sign in its prime. My grandfather was even mentioned by name in the article. Herman had bookmarked the page with an old O.S.O.A. membership card of his. The Occult Sciences of America was like an Elks lodge or the Freemasons, or so I've been told. Herman appeared to be an early member, number 27 to be exact. As far as I knew, the organization dissolved sometime in the early 80s. I know this because my grandfather was a member as well.

She offered to let me keep the field guide but packed up her father's book with his other items. There was an unspoken agreement not to acknowledge what else we had found. She tossed it all into a new box, burying the knife at the bottom. I wondered why Herman, or anyone really, would have such an odd assortment of artifacts. It was clear they were connected to his wife, but the implications were that maybe... maybe, he was hunting the woman he once knew rather than searching for her.

It took us the rest of the day to organize and pack her car. She ended up leaving very little behind, finding even the smallest detail of her father sentimental. With dusk approaching, we said our goodbyes so that she could make it down the mountain before nightfall.

As she pulled out of the driveway, it fully struck me how much she looked like her mother. It may have been the deep-rooted sadness in full display on her face, or how she wore her hair in a way that had been out of style for decades. Either way, it was at that moment that I realized she was better off not knowing of the thing her mother had become. She had already mourned the loss, so there was no point in burdening her with the search that had consumed her father.

I wondered if that knowledge is what pushed him from his daughter, straining their relationship. I could only imagine what he felt each time he looked at her. The resemblance was uncanny. It was only her sloped nose and narrow jaw that set her apart from the woman her father had been waiting for all those years.

I ran the motel without incident in the years after The Family had last left, but it wasn't easy. There was always too much for one person to do in a day, but not enough money coming in to hire help. Some things fell into disrepair while I did my best to handle issues as they happened. The days of preventative maintenance were long gone.

Without many visitors to the mountain, the time between guests was long and lonely. Graham was busy with a remodeling project down at the caverns and spent a lot of time off mountain. He'd stop by on his way up and down the mountain for coffee and a chat, but as the months wore on, those visits came few and far between.

Luckily, I was too busy trying to keep the place afloat to dwell on it. I had my routine and that kept me sane.

Sometimes familiar faces would swing by, but they never stayed long. I began to feel disconnected from the world down the mountain. I needed a break, but it's hard to escape for a vacation when you run the place other people escape to.

Truthfully, what I needed was a distraction. What I got was the next best thing: a reservation from my old friend Gary Edward Ballard. Our last conversation in the lobby had only strengthened our bond. Our shared interest in the lives of strangers, and thus The Family gave us something to bond over. Though we didn't get a chance to chat often, he took to sending postcards every now and then. Because he was always on the move, I was never able to reply, so I saved my stories for his visits, which had become frequent enough for me to consider him a friend.

He had reserved the room online, so I didn't get a chance to catch up with him before his arrival. That was fine because he had booked out a week. We would have plenty of time to talk over coffee. I made up his room and pulled out the nicer sheets and towels. It felt good to go the extra mile. I imagined this excitement was what it felt like for people who prepared rooms for their friends and family when they came to stay for the holidays. Honestly, that's something that gets lost when you do it for a living.

Normally, Gary would arrive in the early afternoon. He was an early riser and preferred driving in the mornings so that he always had time to settle in at his destination. This time, the afternoon came and went without him. The sun was already setting, and he hadn't arrived, so I began to worry. I was checking online for any accident notifications on the mountain when I saw headlights reflect off the wet trees outside.

Gary pulled up in a dented rental car, disheveled and beat from exhaustion. He stepped out with his computer bag draped over his shoulder. He gave me a half-hearted wave, mustering what little energy he had for a smile.

I offered him tea and he accepted. I could tell he needed to sleep, but something was working within his mind that kept him from resting. He paced in the lobby as the kettle steamed. His eyes darted back and forth between the internal lines of dialog in his head. He told me that he hadn't really slept for almost two days. He'd been driving for hours without rest, unwilling to stop anywhere else. He was on edge; he seemed almost afraid.

"Where were you?" I asked, handing him the cup of tea.

He held it for a moment and his mind seemed to wander. "I followed a lead, and I think I may have gone too deep," he said, his eyes drifting above my head, focused somewhere past me.

"Your book?" I queried.

"I... yeah," he said, shaking his head and bringing himself back to the conversation. "I found this place, like the others. They're connected somehow, but I can't figure it out. The only thing I know is that each one leads to the next and every single one is on The Ring of Fire. Each one is at the center of a string of disappearances. Each stop has a geographic history of unsolved cases. Missing people.

Unexplained deaths. Bizarre accidents. Each place has high strangeness in its orbit."

"Where were you?"

"The coast. A hotel. Ocean Point Inn."

A chill ran down my spine. "Why were you there?" I asked, the words tumbling out before I could stop myself.

He looked over, wide-eyed. "What do you know about it?"

I shrugged and told him something adjacent to the truth, "Nothing. I've just heard the name."

He looked at me as if he could tell I was hiding something. His silence spoke volumes. He wanted to know about the secret that was eating away at me. He wanted to know if I knew something more than I let on.

Finally, he asked, "Why did you tell me about The Family?"

"I just... you were the only person that would believe it."

"Have you told others about them?"

I shook my head. "No."

He thought long and hard about his next words, choosing them carefully. He looked me dead in the eye and asked, "Do you think they could be dangerous?"

If I said yes, I would have to explain why. If I had to explain the blood, I'd have to explain why I'd never told anybody. If I had to explain why I never told anyone, I'd have to explain my parents and the deal they made, but I didn't have an answer for that. All I had was incriminating evidence that made me look like an accomplice—that is, if they were in fact dangerous. So instead of telling the full truth, I skirted around it. "They've always been nothing but nice to me. Never caused me any trouble aside from a messy room."

I waited for him to call me out, to ask for the truth, but when he didn't, I questioned him instead. "Why? Do *you* think they could be dangerous?" I hoped he could provide information that I did not have.

He wrestled with the answer. "No... I don't know," he said with an exhale.

"So you believe me then, that they never age?"

"I do. The things I've seen, mostly in the shadows, hints of the unexplainable. All those disappearances. It all makes sense when you look at the bigger picture," he said with an introspective smirk.

"And what is that?" I asked.

"They are all stuck in a time loop. The Ring of Fire is one long, paved Bermuda Triangle. That family never aging, people popping in and out of existence, sightings of inhuman creatures, all of it makes sense if they are unstuck in time."

I was dumbfounded. Sure, I had no better explanation for the possibly immortal guests that checked in every two years, but Gary's hypothesis seemed too out there. Years of normalizing The Family had been hammered into me by my parents, which is probably why I found it difficult to let go of my long-held rationalization: a belief that it was a combination of good genetics and maybe my own poor memory distorting their ages. Beyond that, there was always the most logical explanation: disease. For all I knew, The Little Girl had some sort of disorder where she appeared younger than she actually was. Hell, if it was genetic, it could explain all of them, right? Whatever the true explanation was, I had to believe it was as far from a "time loop" as it was from a family of serial killers.

Gary went on for hours. He told me about his unified theory of high strangeness. It connected everything from Bigfoot and UFOs to déjà vu and geriatric memory loss. He explained that his book had evolved far beyond the true crime novel. It was now something he believed would change the world as we saw it. All he needed was proof. When I pressed him for what that meant, he smiled and waved dismissively.

"I can't tell you that. You're not ready. You'll have to read the book," he replied.

Gary stayed for a few more days and took copious notes on the surrounding area. He tried to visit the closed-down cave system, but even with my connections, he couldn't secure a private tour. He did, however, manage to rope the local Sheriff into meeting him on his way down the mountain.

"Just to get the facts straight. See if it all lines up and get the law's take on the missing people," he told me. He was excited about it.

I wish I had spent more time with Gary on that last day. I wish I had asked him more questions. I wish I hadn't wasted that day reinstalling the online booking software.

Mostly, I regret that the last thing I said to Gary Edward Ballard was "It's a long way down, you should pee before you go."

Gary took my advice and used the restroom one last time after settling up, but we never had a proper goodbye. He hopped into his car and got back on the road. At the time, I expected I'd hear from him in the next few months and maybe then ask the questions I hadn't got around to asking. But when I didn't hear from him, I began to worry. Eventually, I made calls to the numbers he had given in old reservations, but each one had been disconnected. I had no real way of getting a hold of him, so I kept waiting, realizing I'd have to wait for his book to finally be released. That never happened. I even combed the internet for his name and any announcements, but again, nothing came up. The book was never released and Gary never returned. He dropped off the face of the earth, just like the young women he had been researching.

Over time, it ate away at me. He had been so shaken when he arrived, overcome with paranoid delusions. No, that's not right; they weren't delusions. Evil was out there, stalking The Ring of Fire, and he knew it. I was afraid that his pursuit of this evil may have been his undoing. I hurt for the loss of this man that, over time, after years of crossing paths, I had come to consider one of my only friends. Grief gave way to guilt as I began to worry that maybe I had led him to a horrible fate. Maybe it was because he was the only person I'd ever told about The Family. Or maybe it was because isolation had driven me mad, and his paranoia had rubbed off on me.

Eventually, I started searching for mentions of his name in obituaries and news sites. I even checked obscure

Internet forums he'd mentioned once or twice, but he never came up. The last time I saw his name was when he wrote it down on our sign-out sheet.

My weird writer friend who always had time for coffee and a chat had disappeared, like the people he wrote about. With him, I'd lost one more human connection that anchored me to civilization. No matter how long I waited, no matter how much I wanted it, Gary's name would never again pop up on our list of reservations.

The Family, however, were still there, written in red ink on the list of upcoming reservations, because they always came back. Whether I wanted it or not, they always returned. Like clockwork.

I found myself counting down the days until The Family's arrival like a child waiting for Christmas. I'd open the calendar before opening the reservation books. I wasn't exactly looking forward to their visit, but with every day that passed without new guests, I found comfort in the fact that no matter what, they would eventually arrive. In my defense, that desperate anticipation could be chalked up to one very important factor: I was bordering on broke. You see, when the economy and everything else seemed to slow down the previous year, so did travel up the mountain. The caves saw fewer visitors, so budgets were cut. Unfortunately, this led to the park being closed down indefinitely. They had poured so much money into refurbishing the visitor's center the year before, there was nothing left in the budget to fully staff it, especially when the employees routinely outnumbered the guests ten to one, and only ten people worked there. As the world shifted, this remote cave system became less of a priority to the National Park Service. Tourism had waned in the last few years, putting pressure on not only the park but also my own remote business.

With the steadily reduced traffic, it was getting more and more difficult to keep the motel open. I had very little credit, and any loan I could secure would only delay the inevitable for a year or so tops. No bank was willing to take a chance on a dying business in a dead location. It became clear I was going to need to come up with something on my own. The thought of selling crossed my mind, but without a substantial offer, I'd be homeless with no real prospects. Still, even a studio apartment and a dead-end job would at least provide a chance at human interaction. I made plans to visit an agent off-mountain to discuss the possibilities but told him I wasn't holding my breath on an offer.

Things were bleak. My mental health was in the same shape as my bank account, devoid of any real substance or meaning. I needed to figure something out, and fast. I couldn't rely on one reservation that only came every two years.

What I hadn't realized was that my solution had been there the whole time, beneath the register. It actually came as an afterthought. With The Family's imminent arrival, I decided to revisit the first letter and the instructions my parents left for me. As I reread it, the message scrawled on the second envelope popped back into my mind, "Open in case of an emergency; namely, a financial one."

I was immediately frustrated by the fact that I hadn't thought about it sooner. Then again, an actual solution to my hardship was the last thing I could have expected from my parents. Of course I buried it in the back of my mind, alongside all the other promises they never kept. This one was no different because, like everything else my parents left me, it was a gift all wrapped up in a burden.

Inside that second envelope was a letter, same as the first. It instructed me to keep the motel open no matter what, even if the guests stopped coming. There was no room for debate. My parents were very clear that failing to do so would have dire consequences. What were those consequences? Well, they never actually said.

The vague letter then instructed me that in the case of a financial emergency, I was to open one of the brown paper parcels in the safe. I was to do so for no other reason than to keep the motel open and running. So, I opened one.

Beneath the thin, wrinkled paper, wrapped tightly in twine, was a bundle of money. I let out an audible gasp when I realized what it was. Various bills were stacked in no particular order as if collected at random. The amounts were arbitrary, but one bundle alone was enough to carry me through a slow season and there were dozens of them. Despite what the letter said, I opened them all immediately. Each stack of cash was an arbitrary bundle of bills with the newer stacks containing mostly larger denominations.

It was interesting to see the change in designs as I found bills that were older than me.

In fact, the oldest bundles—the ones at the far back of the safe—held currency I barely recognized. It was still American, but it was long out of circulation.

With each bundle I opened, the anxiety over how I was going to survive washed away like footprints on the beach taken by a wave. There was more than enough money for me to start over somewhere else. Even without selling the motel, I had enough to buy a house and live comfortably somewhere off the mountain, among other humans.

With my newfound wealth, I planned to stay open long enough to collect one more bundle from The Family. The most recent one held the largest amount, so it only made sense. Now, I'd be lying if I said the warning of "dire consequences" didn't bother me. I could only assume it involved The Family somehow. However, I didn't plan on sticking around to find out. With that kind of money, I could disappear. With a two-year head start, I doubt they'd ever find me—that is, if they even wanted to. I was nothing to them.

Oh, how easily the human brain accepts the things that make life seem easier.

After the discovery of the cash, I made the decision to close up shop whether I found a buyer for the motel or not. Still, I felt an obligation to retire the family business with a little bit of dignity. The thought of just abandoning it didn't sit right with me. I couldn't just leave it behind like that.

To prepare, I cleaned out all the rooms except The Family's. Nobody had stayed the night in weeks anyway, so I took my time with it. In the year that had passed since Gary's visit, we hadn't had more than one or two rooms occupied at a time. There was something fitting about The Family's room being the last one standing. It was the room that had been repaired the most but, like them, updated the least, with its ruined floorboards, musty carpet, and outdated bathroom. I had always assumed that this, like most other decisions, had been made to appease The Family. There had always been an effort to make that room appear unchanged after all these years. As other rooms were refurnished, that room stayed relatively the same.

The television and some appliances had been updated as they broke, but the carpet and wallpaper stayed like relics in a museum. For the same reason, I suppose, the bathroom remained untouched. Even when there was an issue with the plumbing, my father had refused to call in a professional. Instead, he would insist on fixing it himself using stopgap solutions rather than a total replacement. That was the reason for the sink's perpetually leaky faucet and painted-over rust spots in the bathtub. This room, like those in Gary's theory, appeared to have become unstuck in time. Unlike those rooms, I was ready to move on.

I made one last trek down the mountain to meet with the realtor, an excitable man with an abundance of enthusiasm. The meeting was short and to the point. I brought photos and a small write-up about the motel and its history for the posting. Despite his optimism, he was honest about the fact that anything so far from town would be a hard sell. He mentioned that he had a few buyers in search of some boutique properties, but something in the motel's original deed made it a less-than-ideal purchase. Apparently, permits that allowed us to operate so close to the national park were only valid by way of a grandfather clause, allowing me to inherit the business but not develop it. Essentially, anyone who would buy the land would have to fight tooth and nail to make any substantial upgrades. If I had been in any other situation, this would have been bad news, but selling the property wasn't necessary for me to start my new life. It would have been a nice little bonus, but the thought of leaving The Family to anybody else made me a little uncomfortable.

As I walked back to my car, I chalked it up to the universe preventing me from selling and saddling someone else with my burdens. Worst-case scenario, I could close up the property and let it die a natural death of old age and rot. I wouldn't abandon it. I just wouldn't keep it on life support.

That afternoon I drove out to my favorite breakfast spot for a late brunch. It had been a favorite of mine since I was a child, but my parents would rarely take me. It wasn't malicious; we just didn't spend many mornings at the base of the mountain. We were either passing by early on a road trip or late at night on the way home, and my father was unreasonably anti-"breakfast for dinner".

One of the few times we stopped was on the last drive home from the hospital with my sister. At the time, she was well enough to crave pancakes and wanted nothing more than to stop there for them. I remember my sister giving my father her sausage because, at the time, she wasn't a fan of eating meat. She had a big heart and she didn't like the thought of eating another living animal. Normally my father would've happily taken her sausage and exclaimed, "Great! More for me!" But that time, he didn't say a word. He just cried.

It's weird, the things we can remember, and the things we forget. Small details like the way he wiped his eyes with his napkin are so vivid, yet I couldn't tell you what I ordered or if my mother was even with us on that day. I only remember my father and his tears.

When I got there after my meeting with the realtor, the restaurant was closed. Not just for the day, but forever. It had been so long since I'd been by, I couldn't say when the last time was that I'd seen it open, let alone stopped in. It was just one more relic of my past that had faded away with time. At least I wouldn't miss it when I moved.

I grabbed some fast food and ate in my car. I figured that I might as well get home before dark because even though I knew the roads well, other people didn't. I made it about a quarter of the way up the mountain when my car started to sputter and lurch. I had noticed that the engine sounded rough when the car would idle, but as with most things in my life, I figured I'd get to it eventually. My father was always very good about car stuff, making sure he always had gas, the tires were always good, and any odd noise was looked at the next time he was in town. For a while, I had tried to do the same, but isolation and apathy had long since drained away my proactive impulses.

My car came to a stop halfway up the mountain, only about a mile down from the cave entrance, but by road, it was quite a distance. The cliffside was so steep that the road wound for miles before looping back. I was so close, but oh so far.

I called for a tow truck, but the combination of a busy day and my remote location meant that a driver wouldn't make it until after dark. I had a lot of time to kill and not a lot to kill it with.

Spotty service and a dying phone battery meant I'd have to find something analog to pass the time. While the way up was rather steep, I happened to break down at a rather flat spot on the mountain. There was a turn-off within walking distance where tourists would stop for photos. With nothing else to do, I decided I'd at least check it out while I still had some daylight.

Not a single car passed me on my walk along the shoulder, but I still crossed the highway as fast as I could. The gravel turnout was wide. Back in the day, you could find a dozen cars parked here with families milling about, stretching their legs.

Near the back, next to an ancient wooden picnic table, I discovered a small wooden post near a trailhead named "Murmur" that I had no idea existed. The small path cut through a narrow crack in the mountain lined with lush green shrubs. I'd driven by so many times but never noticed it. I still had an hour and a half of daylight, so I ventured forth into the broken cliffside. It was less of a hike and more of a short walk into a tight squeeze where the mountain converged. Still, I quickly understood why people made a point to stop. Up above me, I could see small openings and caves, like Swiss cheese in the stone. As the wind blew in, the crevice carried it up and past the openings, making a low, haunting whistling sound. Like a murmur. The trail's name was actually pretty clever. The closer I got to the end of the trail, the more intense the wind seemed to blow as it bottlenecked and billowed up. The "murmurs" made by the caves grew louder and more chaotic. The strange sound was unlike anything I'd ever heard before. I swore at times I could hear a voice calling out from somewhere far above.

"Pleaasssseeeee," the wind begged in a long drawn-out whisper.

I stood there and listened, long enough for the sun to disappear, lost behind the horizon and hidden by the twisting wall of the trail.

I felt a cold chill the moment the sun no longer touched my skin, and I decided I'd better hurry back to the car. I had only made it a few steps when the wind picked up and the voice returned. "Come baaaaaccccckkk," it begged me.

I stopped and looked up at the cliffside, jagged with shadow and hidden from sunlight. Another gust crept up the back of my shirt and I shuddered. Somewhere above, I thought I caught a glimpse of movement near a small cave. My rational mind told me it was an animal, maybe a bird, or something carried by the wind. Obscured by dusk, I couldn't be sure what it was I saw up there. In a small pocket on the otherwise smooth rock, fifty feet above me on the ledge, something leaned out and looked down. What little light was left was reflected back at me, like you'd see in the eyes of a nocturnal predator. Without hesitation, I ran.

"Nooooooo," the wind called after me as I sprinted through the narrow path.

I looked back one more time, but my view was obstructed by the angle of the rock. Still, I felt its presence, watching me.

Imagined or not, whatever it was I'd heard and seen was not something I wanted to confront.

I sprinted across the highway without looking, narrowly avoiding the tow truck that was on its way to rescue me.

He slammed on his brakes and I slipped onto the rocky shoulder.

"I'm so sorry!" he screamed from the window.

"No, my fault," I yelled back as I dusted the gravel off my pants. After an awkward moment of silence, I added, "I'm right over there. That's me," and pointed to my car.

The driver met me on the shoulder and was already under the hood by the time I walked up. He parked right behind me and put out some reflective cones to give us a small sense of safety on an otherwise very dangerous road.

I held his flashlight for him as he ran the diagnostics on my car using a portable device. We made some small talk about how long it took him to reach me and how often he was up here towing cars that had been caught in a landslide. None of it made me feel particularly good about standing there in the dark, even with the cones and the flashlight.

"I think I got some good news," he said with a smile, unplugging the device.

"You're driving me home?"

"Better. You can probably drive yourself. When was the last time you changed your spark plugs?" he asked, heading back to his truck.

"Honestly, not sure. I don't drive much."

He rustled around for a bit in the back seat. "I can tell."

"Do I need new ones?"

He popped out with two plugs in hand and a small brush. "Yeah, probably sooner than later. Two are in pretty bad shape but the rest just need a good cleaning. I got two on hand, but you'll want to replace them all when you get a chance."

The whole fix took less than ten minutes, and I was back on the road after tipping the guy with every loose bill I had in my wallet. On the drive home, I thought about how if this had happened anywhere else, I would have just walked to a coffee shop and waited while sipping a cappuccino. I was sick of living such a secluded life where even the smallest inconvenience quickly became a full-scale hassle. Still, there was something about the mountain that had kept me here. Like that voice in the wind, it always called me back and then begged me to stay.

"No more," I said to myself. "I'm done with it."

It was only a matter of time before they would arrive, and with their departure, I'd finally be able to leave this all behind. All I needed was to check out The Family one last time.

As I changed the sheets for the last time before The Family's arrival, I relished the thought of never doing so again. The task itself seemed less tedious with the promise of such finality. There was a sense of excitement as I vacuumed the old, matted carpet and fluffed the pillows that would barely see any use.

During the days leading up to their reservation, I was ready for them to arrive, but even more so, I was ready for them to leave. That was probably why everything seemed to hang in limbo.

But then, the arrival date that had been circled in red by my father long before he died came and went. On the first day, I thought nothing of it. I chalked it up to a mis-calculation on my father's part or, hell, bad traffic. On the second day, I decided to check back on older reservations to see if they had ever been late before. As it turned out, they hadn't. As far back as our records went, The Family had always arrived on time. It came as a relief when on the third day—or night, rather—the sound of their ancient exhaust rattled into the parking lot.

When The Family arrived, three days late, I could already tell something was off. It was clear the moment they emerged from the car that something tragic had happened, though you wouldn't have known from their usual unemotional demeanor. Black soot clung to the white flaked paint of their car and two of the rear windows had been smashed and left open to the elements. Furthermore, what I had always known as a family of seven arrived as six. One of the teenagers, the boy, was not with them. Of course, this was not acknowledged by anyone upon check-in.

Any sense of emotional connection I'd made last time was gone. The Little Girl stayed beside The Teenage Girl, never once asking about my mother. Still, her hollow eyes were fixed on the door to our kitchen. There was an empathy in her that her family lacked, or maybe rejected. I could only imagine they insisted she dampen it as well.

They arrived very late, almost morning, so I saw very little of them after they checked in. As usual, they stayed in their room for the following day with the heavy blackout curtains pulled shut.

The sun had barely slipped behind the mountain when their door opened. The Old Man emerged, already smoking. His gaze was fixed on the highway, as if he were watching for something, waiting. He spent most of that first night chain-smoking outside their door while the rest of The Family stayed inside. A sentry on watch. What he was looking for wasn't clear to me, but he stood there, observing the night, waiting.

On the second night, The Old Man emerged again, cigarette in hand. I only noticed him because I heard the faint click of their room door closing. With so little activity around the motel, every sound was noticeable. He seemed to carry with him a weight on his shoulders, visible in the way he slouched. It felt odd to see him burdened by something.

The Teenage Girl joined The Old Man sometime around eight in the evening. Together they watched the road with an unsettling focus. If they exchanged words, I didn't notice. If they moved, I couldn't tell. I was exhausted after sleeping through most of the day, which only added another layer to the brain fog. My circadian rhythm suffered from the three-day disruption in my sleep schedule. Three days of waiting for them to arrive. Now, with nothing else to do, I spent my time in the office, sitting by the window, occasionally peeking out to observe, careful not to be seen.

At some point, well after midnight, I had gone to make a pot of coffee. I figured that if I embraced their nocturnal ways, I'd need fuel. When I returned with my warm mug, I noticed the girl had left, so I moved over to the other window for a different vantage point. I pulled back the curtain just in time to see The Teenage Girl stepping into the woods, out on the other side of the highway. I waited for a bit, alternating windows, watching for any movement from The Old Man or the return of The Teenage Girl, but I saw neither. He stood motionless and she stayed hidden among the trees. Eventually, boredom took hold and I busied myself with other tasks, things I'd been putting off. If the girl returned that night, I didn't notice. The Old Man, though, never wavered in his watch. With only a few hours until sunrise, my eyes began to blur, and my lids grew heavy. Despite my best efforts to stay awake, sleep came with such a heavy hand that I couldn't resist. What was supposed to be a quick nap to rest my eyes became a few hours of sleep on the lobby couch.

I woke up in the early morning, warm from the sun coming through the window. As expected, The Old Man was gone. I did my best to fall back asleep, but my mind wouldn't allow it. I spent the rest of my day decluttering in preparation for my move. Once the sun shifted past noon, I had a light meal of leftover pasta I'd made two days before. I showered, changed, and steeped in the prospect of a new life ahead. The plan was to stay up all night, but the sandman visited me late in the afternoon, shortly before the sun was down. Despite my best efforts, I once again fell asleep in the lobby.

I was awoken by a quiet knock at the door. Outside I could hear the gentle patter of rain. The door cracked open.

"Hello?" said a voice, cracked and gritty, but still youthful.

A young man, wearing expensive but dirty outdoorsman clothing and a large hiking backpack stepped inside. I composed myself and hurried to the desk, "Sorry, come on in. I was... I must have drifted off," I apologized.

Brushing water off his rain-resistant jacket, he asked with a hint of undue embarrassment, "You got any vacancies?"

I found myself checking the computer even though I knew the rest of the rooms were no longer guest-ready. "Are you parked outside?"

He double-checked his appearance as he made his way to the gas fireplace. "No, I walked. I'm a little lost actually, and the pigs around here are real fucking dodgy."

"Pigs, up here?"

"Cops..."

"Oh, we only have the Sheriff up here. And the park rangers."

"Sheriff then, I guess. Whatever. Either way, dude was following me for almost two miles. Hassled me when I tried to camp on a pull-off."

"Must have been the rangers then. Graham is a stickler for camping rules."

"Who?" he asked, with a look that teenagers give anyone over the age of twenty-five.

"My friend Graham is the local ranger. Big green hat. He's about yay big..." I said, gesturing to his height.

"Naw, you were right. Sheriff. Green hat rangers are always cool, this dude wasn't. Total cop hat."

"How old are you?" I asked, realizing how young he truly looked. The grime from weeks without a shower had darkened his already sun-baked skin and emphasized the cracks and creases. His cheeks were sunken from self-induced malnutrition and his clothes were tattered and patched. I could tell he was still a child because, despite all of this, he still looked happy. He embraced the hardship with wild abandon as only an optimistic youth could.

"I'm eighteen," he chuckled. "Step by step, I'm checking out what this country has to offer before I enlist to protect it. I've been camping a lot, but it's pretty wet tonight. Between the rain and the Sheriff, I'm just really tired."

"Sorry, that's a long trek up here. But, unfortunately, we don't have anything open." I apologized. "We're actually in the process of..."

The door creaked open, startling us both. The Teenage Girl stood on the threshold, the rain behind her.

"We have space," she said, her eyes fixed on the young man as her hands combed through her long greasy hair. Her white cotton dress was immaculate without a single wrinkle to be seen. I realized she was somehow dry as a bone.

"The other rooms have been gutted. Their room is the only one that is still furnished," I said, watching the two of them gaze longingly at each other as if I were no longer in the room. The boy seemed transfixed, if not by her beauty, then by something else.

"Then it is settled," she said, her eyes locked on his.

"Well, I suppose I could set up a cot in here," I offered, wanting him to stay anywhere but with her.

"How... how much?" the boy stuttered.

She took his hand and led him to the door. "No need. Come with me. The linens are clean."

"Are you sure?" I asked her. But really, my question was directed at him.

Neither she nor the young man bothered to reply. My gut felt hollow and guilt flooded in. I wanted to stop him, but I knew there was nothing I could do, not really.

He followed her outside. The rain had ceased, and a cold chill blew into the lobby. The boy closed the door behind himself without so much as a glance in my direction. I felt like a ghost haunting my own home. It was an unsettling feeling, something I hoped I'd never feel ever again.

I watched them chat outside. From the window, I could see all the way to The Family's room. They walked slowly and he was animated in his questions, while The Teenage Girl remained focused forward, barely turning to look at him. She had him in her pocket, like a siren to lonely young men. He was powerless against it, as most men his age would be.

After a slow, casual stroll, they reached the room, and she led him inside. When she closed the door, I noticed the rain return as if it were no longer being held back by her mere presence. I sat in my chair and from my new vantage point, I could see into the parking lot.

My heart skipped a beat at the sight of The Old Man standing alone at the center of the crumbling asphalt lot. He looked unimpressed—no, agitated. His usually stoic eyes were narrowed and focused on the door of his room. I watched him for nearly thirty minutes, and in that time he did not move, not even an inch.

When the door to that room opened again, the boy emerged, changed, showered, and laughing. The Teenage Girl followed him out, giggling. It was unsettling to see that kind of emotion on display. She was almost unrecognizable.

I watched them for over an hour with a strange protective urge to keep an eye on the boy. I couldn't help but wonder how the rest of The Family reacted upon hearing he would stay with them. The Old Man had wandered off, no longer standing at the center of the parking lot, but I had an odd feeling he wasn't far. I could almost sense his presence, hidden among the trees, watching from a distance.

The young couple laughed and flirted and one of them produced a cigarette, though I'm not certain it was tobacco. They smoked and I watched her inch closer to him. I couldn't help but think of how weird it was for them to be canoodling like that with her family inside and The Old Man not far off. God knows I would never have tried that when I was their age. I mean, his age. Who knows what her age was, though I'm almost certain it wasn't even close to his.

It was clear he wasn't lying when he said that he was tired. I watched him slowly drift off, fighting the urge to end their "date" early. Eventually, he gave in to the exhaustion and excused himself. She fawned over him and laughed as he waved goodbye and went inside.

The moment the door closed, her emotions drained out. Before my eyes, she went from smiling to stoic so fast that if emotional whiplash were a thing, I felt it at that moment. In the span of an exhale, she was back to her familiar soulless self. She stood and walked into the parking lot. The Old Man emerged from the shadows to meet her. They were far enough away that it was difficult to hear exactly what either said, but with the window open, I could make out a few select words when one of them raised their voice. They were arguing, but unlike him, she remained outwardly calm. It came to a head in an explosion of untapped emotion. The Old Man's rigid body craned forward, seemingly growing taller and towering over The Teenage Girl. The amber lamps in the parking lot reflected like fire in his eyes as he yelled loud enough for me to hear him.

"He is NOT a replacement!" The Old Man bellowed between heaving breaths.

The small Teenage Girl did not flinch. She then said something to him, quiet and calm. I couldn't hear it, the distance between us swallowing up her words, a reminder that I was nothing more than a voyeur peering in on their argument.

The Old Man steadied himself, trying not to shout, but his voice still boomed, "He may still come..." There was a waiver to his words, betraying his emotions. I had seen more intensity in these two in one night than I had in my entire life.

Gently, she placed her hand on his cheek and spoke, but again, I could not hear her.

His voice cracked with pained concern. "We can't go back. Melprice is ash."

The word Melprice rang in my ears, conjuring memories of my youth. It was the name of the town where my aunt had lived. Why were they talking about Melprice?

At some point I noticed The Middle Aged Man lurking near their car. Like me, he observed from a distance, unseen by the other two. I'm not sure where he was before, but it was clear their argument had drawn him in.

Both of us watched as the other two stood in silence. The Teenage Girl waited as The Old Man calmed himself and slowly returned to his phlegmatic self. Once he had composed himself, she touched his cheek. He nodded in understanding. She then turned and walked back to the room.

As she passed The Middle Aged Man, still lingering by the car, he said something to her. She stopped, but as far as I could tell, she didn't respond. The Middle Aged Man shot a pleading glance to The Old Man standing beneath the amber lights. The Old Man shook his head and for the briefest moment, appeared sympathetic. Agitated, the girl motioned for them to follow her inside, leaving the door open behind her. With his head hung low, The Middle Aged Man followed her.

The Old Man, though, did not follow. Instead, he turned back towards the road, lit a cigarette, and waited. A gargoyle keeping watch over the mountain road.

Once again, I watched The Old Man until sleep took hold and pulled me under.

* * *

In the morning, I awoke to the sun on my face, burning through the blinds. I made myself coffee and took a long shower. I followed through with my morning routine and pushed the cleaning cart past their room. I stopped at their door and listened, despite the fact that they were always dead silent during the day. I heard the quiet hum of daytime television and the tired shuffle of someone inside. I considered knocking, but thought better of it and went back to my office. I was achingly curious, but years of customer service had taught me not to intrude.

I remembered suddenly, the night before and the word that stuck with me: Melprice. It had been years since I had spoken with my aunt. I found her number in my father's old Rolodex, still open to her name from reaching out when my mother's passed. I had left a message, but she never bothered to return the call.

I dialed the number and let it ring. There was no answer, no machine. I checked that third envelope, but the number scribbled on it was the same. I planned to call again later in the afternoon, but I knew the day would likely get away from me; other things had already begun to take up that space in my mind.

The loud thud of a room's door closing ordered my attention. I hung up the phone and raced to the window. For the first time in weeks, I heard another human in the daytime. I watched as the young hiker from the night before walked across the parking lot to the ice maker.

I felt a deep-seated need to talk to him, to ask him questions I couldn't ask The Family. I rushed outside, trying to appear calm and cool, but I waved frantically trying to get his attention.

He noticed me and cocked his head to the side with concern or confusion or maybe it was both.

"That ice maker needs to be cleaned. Ice tastes like dust!" I shouted across the parking lot.

He stopped in his tracks, unsure of how to respond.

I pointed back to the office, "We have a smaller one in the kitchen, but it tastes better. How much do you need?"

He shrugged. "A bucket, I suppose."

I waved for him to follow, and he did. I tried to act casual as he jogged to catch up to me. "How'd you sleep?" I asked.

Once he reached my side, he smiled and said, "Great! My first bed in a few weeks."

I stopped and turned to him. "They gave you the bed?"

He looked confused. He glanced back at the room, then back to me. "Yeah, not sure where they slept. We dozed off watching T.V. and when I woke up, she was gone. Old guy never came back either. I sleep pretty heavy though, so I don't know."

I had always assumed they still slept on the beds, just, not under the sheets. But if they didn't, then where? Where did they sleep? It was such an odd thought anyway, picturing them fully clothed, piled on the beds. I tried to play off my mild bewilderment and started walking again. "What about the others, though?"

"What others?" he asked.

I didn't want to sound crazy, so I changed the subject. "Oh, they must have checked out," I said as we walked past The Family's car, still parked outside. "Speaking of, when are you leaving?"

I could hear him deciding on the spot, "Tonight probably. I like walking at night"

We reached the door to the office, and I held it open for him. As he passed, I asked, "Isn't that dangerous?"

He chuckled and stood aside to let me show him the way. "Naw, I got reflective tape on my bag and stuff. And I got a knife. I'm good."

I didn't want to press him any more than I already had, so I maneuvered the conversation to his travels and asked more about his journey. We filled his ice bucket, and he told me about everyone he had met on his way. I walked him all the way back to the room, listening. He produced the room key and opened the door. I tried my best to remain inconspicuous as I looked over his shoulder, inside. Sure enough, the room was empty. He was alone.

"Hey, you're okay, right?" I blurted out.

"Yeah, why? What do you mean?" he chuckled.

"I just, I want to know that everything in there was... safe. They're strangers."

He cocked his head to the side and let out another confused chuckle. "So are you though, right? Everyone's a stranger until you get to know them."

"And you got to know them?" I asked.

He shrugged. "Not really."

I could tell I was making him uncomfortable, so I dropped it.

We said our goodbyes and as he was about to shut the door, he pulled it open again, "I never asked. How much is the room? I want to offer to split it."

"Already paid for," I told him. "I'm sure it's fine."

He accepted with a thankful head nod and quick smile before retreating inside.

I went back to the office and locked up. Even though they rarely requested help with anything, I put up a sign saying I had stepped out for a break and to ring the doorbell if they needed me. The bell had been rigged by my grandfather to ring throughout our house in the case of a late-night guest or an after-hours visit. I then set my alarm for sundown and decided to take a nap. This was their last evening and I wanted to be well-rested for their check-out. Like graduation or a wedding, this felt like a big life event, but without the excitement. I fell asleep the moment my head hit the pillow and I dreamed of what my life would be like, free from the shackles of the mountain.

The doorbell never rang and I slept until my alarm went off. The gauzy pink-orange of a cotton candy sunset greeted me through my bedroom window. I got dressed and readied myself for the last check-out I would ever need to do. After they left, I would have nothing holding me back and enough money to start over.

Still, I couldn't help but worry for the hitchhiker. The Family seemingly disappeared after the argument in the parking lot, and it filled me with an uneasy feeling of dread. Surely, the boy would have noticed them leaving, or at the very least, the return of the two older men. Then again, if he was as tired as he looked, he could have been lost in the heavy dreams of deep sleep and missed their presence. The thought of him sleeping as they hovered over him sent a shiver down my spine. Still, where could they have gone? If they weren't in the room... where were they?

Before the sun fully set, I made my way over to the room. The Family's car was still parked, unmoved from the night before. I felt irrational for worrying, but the image of the blood-stained carpets I had replaced over the years tugged at my conscience. The closer I got to the room, the more my anxiety hissed like static in my head. I was ready to knock and, if nobody answered, I was ready to let myself in, but just four feet from the door, out stepped the hitchhiker. He smiled and waved.

"Oh, sorry, I was just coming by to... clean. How was... your stay?" I asked awkwardly.

He closed the door behind him, adjusted his large backpack, covered in reflective tape, and grunted, "Great. Thanks for everything!"

"Be safe," I said, standing outside the room.

"Will do. If you see her, please thank her again."

As I watched him go, something in the woods caught my eye, a subtle shadow of movement behind the tree line. The hitchhiker must have caught it too because he stopped as he reached the road. We both watched the dark woods for movement, but as the sun set, it became almost impossible.

The sudden snap of a twig startled us and a deer emerged from the trees. Its eyes met mine and the hitchhiker turned to see me still standing there. The deer then turned quickly and leaped back into the woods. The boy gave me one last half-hearted wave goodbye and disappeared around the bend of the road.

Once again, I felt a heavy sense of isolation. I wondered where The Family had gone, and if they would return to check out. My questions were answered with a strange wooden thud coming from somewhere in the room. I heard the analog click of the television being turned on and the sudden commotion of people moving inside. Clearly, they had returned to see the boy off, but that made his final request very strange. Once again, their mere presence was shrouded in mystery. More than ever, I was glad to see the boy go.

Without a reason to knock, I left them alone in the room. I returned to the office to wait. More than ever, I was ready for them to check out, ready for them to leave... forever.

From behind my desk, I waited with a mug of tea and listened to the soft crackle of the only public radio station that reached the mountaintop. It was a lighthearted radio story about a wedding ruined by a bad case of catered buffet food poisoning. I was only halfway through when I heard something troubling outside. An ear-piercing shriek erupted from the woods, making the hairs on my neck stand on end. I quickly turned off the radio and listened through the low rush of winds outside. Another long, pained moan echoed from the tree line. For a moment, my mind convinced me it was the wind, but it was followed by an unnatural screech of tortured agony.

A strange shrill echo made it impossible to decipher what kind of creature made the horrifying sound. Another blood-curdling scream was cut short, making the whole ordeal even more unsettling.

I wanted to step outside to see if I could hear more, but my instincts took hold and kept me rooted in the chair behind my desk. Still, I drew back the curtain to see what I could. There was nothing but light fog and halos of light in the parking lot.

Moments later, The Old Man emerged from the darkness. He looked across the road towards the motel and if I didn't know better, I'd say he looked directly at me. He dragged something large and burdensome behind him. The object was low to the ground and hidden by the brush. Without pause, The Old Man crossed the paved highway, pulling whatever it was in his wake. The large dark mass looked to be half his size, but he dragged it with ease. Inches from the reach of the parking lot lights, I thought I caught a reflection of something in it. Without explanation, I felt a sudden rush of cool air around me and the always-inconsistent light that lit the parking lot flickered out.

In the strobe of amber flashing, I watched The Old Man trudge across the asphalt, trailed by the hulking mass and leaving a dark wet streak behind him. I watched for as long as I dared, but once he was close enough to notice me, I hid. Unfortunately, this was not close enough for me to make out what the object was. Crouched behind my desk, I heard him open the car door. He rummaged around inside, between brief pauses of quiet. The door slammed shut and moments later, I heard the door to their room close with a heavy thud. The parking lot light stopped flickering and illuminated everything, casting light on the wall above my head. Still, I did not dare look. I know now that I was too afraid of seeing something I couldn't unsee.

In my heart, I knew exactly what it was. Even if I wasn't ready to admit it to myself.

The next sound was that of the rain on the asphalt, washing away whatever it was that trailed behind The Old Man. I could have gone out to investigate, but I didn't. Instead, I stayed behind that desk, waiting for them to check out one last time.

An hour or so later, the heavy rain had passed, but a thick fog had moved in, covering the mountain. I couldn't see much further than where the sidewalk ended. The rest of the parking lot and their room might as well have been a million miles away.

The Family packed up their car under the veil of fog that hung in the parking lot outside their room, so when the time came for them to check out, I was caught by surprise. I hadn't eaten a proper meal since The Family had arrived, so I had gone into the kitchen to grab myself something to eat. When I walked back into the office with a nearly expired cup of yogurt, The Old Man was standing silently at the desk. Behind him, the rest of The Family gathered near the door.

"We are leaving," he stated.

I put down my yogurt and opened the ledger. He slid the keys across the wood desk from his jacket pocket and pulled out a brown paper parcel wrapped in twine.

"I'm sorry to say this, but your family will officially be the last guests we host here," I explained, trying to break the news casually as I typed into the computer. Part of me regretted even bringing it up.

The man stared at me blankly. The Little Girl standing behind him looked up at The Teenage Girl, but she did not react. The Little Girl then looked back at me with an odd sense of worry on her face.

The man did not seem upset, nor happy about it. As always, he was emotionless.

"Sure," he said with an unnerving fake smile.

With that, he turned to leave. The Family followed, but The Little Girl pulled away from the teenager. She stood there staring at me for a long time as everyone left.

"You better hurry," I said, pointing at her family as the door closed behind them, trying to break the awkwardness that clearly only I felt.

"Do you not remember me?" she asked.

"Of course, I do. How could I not?" I replied.

I could see The Old Man out in the parking lot as the fog drifted. I watched him notice The Little Girl's absence as he reached the car. Without urgency, he left the car door open and came to retrieve her.

As he approached the office door, The Little Girl stepped closer to the desk.

"If you aren't here when we return, they will leave me. They will put me back in the caves and never return," she whispered.

"What do you mean?" I asked, my mind racing.

"I'm too young. She says I'm a mistake. She regrets turning me..." Her words were cut off by the opening of the door.

Again, I felt that unspoken bond.

The Old Man stood in the doorway, his gaze fixed on The Little Girl. Neither of them said a word. The Little Girl left with him without resistance, but not before giving me one more pleading glance. As The Middle Aged Man carried the last bag from the room, I saw The Little Girl run past him back inside, squeezing past the door before it closed. Everybody else was in the car and ready to leave before The Little Girl emerged, shutting the door behind her. She then shot me a pleading glance, as if she were asking me something but couldn't say the words.

As their car pulled out of the parking lot, I could see her in the back window, watching me as they drove away.

Once they were gone, I waited to clean the room. Even though it would be my last time cleaning up someone else's mess, I was in no hurry to face whatever disgusting state they had left the bathroom in. All I could think of was the heaping mass The Old Man dragged out of the woods. Instead, I counted the bundle of cash left in the paper parcel. It was enough to carry me two seasons, but more so, along with the rest still in the safe, it was enough to start a new life.

I opened a bottle of wine and drank half before grabbing the cleaning supplies. I knew what kind of gore awaited me in that bathroom. At least this time, I wouldn't have to replace the carpet. It didn't need to be pristine, it just needed to not raise red flags if somebody came to buy the motel. Either way, this was it, my last time scrubbing someone else's soap scum and body fluid... and blood. I closed the ledger for the last time and savored the moment, knowing I'd never have to open it again.

When I finally made it to the old room, it was morning. I opened the door and the rising sun cast a light across the neatly made beds and overstuffed ashtray. As I walked toward the bathroom, something on the bed caught my eye.

Laid neatly on one of the unused pillows was a photograph. I put down my cleaning supplies and picked up the photo. It was torn on one side, so it was only half of the picture. It shouldn't have been shocking, but it did catch me off guard. They had left things before, but this felt...intentional.

The photo was of two young children. One was a young girl in a floral dress, the same Little Girl that had left with The Family. Despite the faded age of the photo, she looked the exact same. It may have been the half-bottle of wine, but for some reason, the child she was holding hands with didn't register. Or maybe it was denial. Either way, I was staring at the photo for far too long before I recognized the other child — myself. I was the child she was holding hands with.

It made sense though, since I'm sure we had known each other our whole lives. There was nothing unusual about me in the photo, except maybe how happy I looked. She, on the other hand, seemed somehow different. It took me a moment to realize what was off about her, but when I did, I gasped. She was younger. Not much younger than she appeared now, but slightly younger than I had seen her in decades.

It was clear that the photo was taken here at the motel, outside of the office beneath the sign that read, "You're always welcome." I recognized the background, not only because it was a familiar space, but because I had seen this pose somewhere else.

Then it clicked.

I abandoned the cleaning and ran back to the office with the photo in hand. Hung above the fireplace, across from the desk was a collection of photos my mother had curated over the years. Ones she still allowed. It was mostly my parents and me, but there were also snapshots of famous guests or old regulars. There were still none of my sister. I ran my fingers over the torn edge of the photo of myself and The Little Girl and I remembered one specific photo that hung over the fireplace. It was small and oddly shaped, but it was my mother's favorite because of how happy my father and her looked. It was just the two of them standing outside the office beneath half the sign, same as me and

The Little Girl. They were smiling. It was taken in the same spot but slightly off to the right, while we stood to the left.

I ripped the photo of my parents off the wall and broke the frame, too impatient to be delicate. I pulled the small odd-shaped photo from the frame and confirmed my suspicion. It was torn.

I held the photo of my parents up with the photo of The Little Girl and myself. They were two halves of the same photograph.

And though I couldn't remember her face, I knew immediately who The Little Girl was. I held the photo close to my nose and breathed in deeply. Soft Lavender.

Suddenly, it all began to fall into place. She was my older sister. I now understood the deal my parents had made with The Family. My knees went weak, and I dropped to the floor, unable to contain the sob that tore through my body. A pained haunting wail, vaguely human, hung in the room like a storm siren. As the tears wet my cheeks, I realized the sound was coming from me.

I'd already made my decision before my sister left the photograph. The plans were already in motion, and it seemed as if closing the motel was inevitable. I'd never really wanted the family burden to begin with. The increasingly isolated life I was leading only reinforced my desire to leave. The sudden revelation of my sister being alive was not going to be enough to keep me there. Family had anchored me to that spot for too long and I owed it to myself to move on. As for my sister, she had survived without me for longer than I could remember, so there was nothing I could offer her. I wanted to forget her final words to me, the threat that she would be left behind. I wasn't even sure I could trust her. She was essentially a stranger, a ghost of someone I once loved. Two things were very clear though.

First, whatever she was, she was no longer human, not in the traditional sense anyway. Second, she was not my responsibility. I was not going to change course now. I had decided to move forward with selling the motel.

At one point, the gentleman I had hired to do the listing called me after typing up the description. "That place has really been in your family that long?" he asked.

"Three generations of changing sheets and renting rooms."

"And you're sure you want to give it up?"

"As much as I love handling a stranger's soiled sheets, yes. I am finally ready," I told him.

I was going to leave it all behind: The Family, the business, the blood. I was done with it all. I was finally ready to move on.

And then he arrived.

I hadn't bothered to clean their room after The Family had left. I was too emotionally drained to take on the daunting task. Two things were always inevitable: they always paid in cash, and the bathroom was always left just shy of a crime scene. So, instead of dealing with it, I retreated into the house and surrounded myself with memories.

I went to the freezer and dug out ground meat my father had frozen and forgotten about. Unless you hunt, fresh meat is a luxury for us mountain folk. Freezer burn was a familiar flavor in our household. With the last bag of pasta left in the pantry, I made a meal that my mother used to make for my sister: spaghetti and meatballs with home-made garlic toast. It was comforting.

I finished off the bottle of wine with dinner.

The heavy meal and sobering revelation that my sister was still alive kept my head from spinning. Any buzz I had felt was gone by the time I cleared the table. I was elbow-deep in dishwater when I heard the front door rattle as if someone were trying to get in. The old service bell at the front desk suddenly rang. I dried my hands and listened for them to announce their presence. The vacancy sign had long been extinguished and the front door to the office had been locked after The Family left. Whoever had rung the bell, they had not been welcomed in by me.

I opened the door slowly, with the kitchen knife gripped tight in my hand.

"I'm sorry. We're closed," I warned them.

The door swung open to an empty room, the bell still resonating on the desk.

"I am late," said a deep voice from the darkest corner of the room, behind the reach of the fireplace's gentle light.

The figure looked like an animal cowering in the corner, balled up and small. They were more of an unkempt shape than a human, covered in mud and grime.

When the figure finally stood, I saw how bad they looked. The dirt reached every crevice as if they were buried in it, and only the whites of their eyes stood out from the black coat of mud. It was a boy. He was thin and emaciated, but still, there was a strength about him.

"I'm sorry, but we're closed," I repeated.

"But the sign…" he said, pointing up at "You're Always Welcome" hanging outside the window.

"That, uh… We don't have any clean rooms. I'm sorry. You'll have to find somewhere else," I said, feeling a sudden sense of discomfort. For a moment I thought, maybe he was the hitchhiker and had gotten lost and returned, but his voice wasn't familiar. It wasn't him.

The boy's white eyes met mine with a stare so intense it felt as if he were looking straight through me.

"But we already have a room," he said. His voice was soft yet commanding and wholly devoid of emotion. It was then that I recognized him, not by his voice but by his presence.

He was The Teenage Boy from The Family, though thinner than I remembered. His familiar young features were hidden, caked in filth, but I knew it was him.

"Have they departed?" he asked.

I nodded.

"Have they left me anything?" he asked, his voice finally cracking.

I didn't know how to answer. I wasn't sure what he meant.

"Have they left any behind?" He said, sounding suddenly desperate.

"I don't know," I replied, pulling the room keys from their hook. "But you are welcome to check."

He took the keys from my hands, his eyes lingering on my arm. It was as if he saw something I did not.

"Thank you," he said, unlocking the office door before slipping outside and trailing mud behind him.

It wasn't until he was gone that I realized the caked footprints of mud and ash only led outside.

That night, I couldn't sleep. I watched his room from my window and waited for him to leave, but once he closed that door, he disappeared inside. He never even turned on the light.

I only left my perch long enough to make coffee, but even then, I listened for the creak of that heavy old door. Thankfully, I never did hear it.

Looking out on that empty parking lot, it dawned on me that he was what The Old Man was waiting for every night. I recalled the heated conversation between him and the other teenager. My worry now was that they would return for him. All I wanted was to be done with them, so the sooner he left, the better. Everything was so fresh with my sister, I wasn't ready to face her just yet. I needed time, and the longer he was here, the less I had. I figured one night was enough to get cleaned up and rest. I'd do my best to usher him out, anywhere but here.

When daylight came, I realized that there was no car outside. He had either hitched or walked up the mountain. However he made it, I don't believe it was safe or easy. Still, he needed to go.

I decided to check on him. There was something about the sunlight that made me feel safer when I was around The Family. After The Teenage Boy's peculiar arrival last night, I wasn't taking any chances. I knocked many times and announced my intent to enter if he did not answer. He did not respond.

The door opened with that familiar old creak and the sun crept into the dark room. Cigarette smoke hung heavy in the air and danced in the beams of light. The room key sat idle next to the ashtray.

"Hello?" I said.

The room appeared empty, but I traced his muddy tracks from the door to the table, then to the bathroom. Like his idol James Dean, he had smoked the old butts left by the others so that nothing but burnt filters remained. The beds, again, were untouched.

I knocked gently on the bathroom door.

"Are you okay?" I asked.

The carpet sloshed underfoot, wet from the bathroom overflow.

"I'm coming in..." I announced, turning the knob.

As the bathroom door opened inward, it pushed aside a layer of sticky wet sludge. It was a mixture of deep red and earthen brown.

The putrid sweet smell of decay hit before my eyes could comprehend the horror of what lay before me.

The bathtub was half filled with thick old blood and clumps of mud left behind by the boy. His clothes were piled in a damp muddy heap outside the bath. The floor was sticky with blood and dirt. The boy was nowhere to be seen.

I stepped inside. The bathtub was full enough with that gruesome sludge that something could still be hiding beneath the surface. As I had done many times before, I rolled up my sleeve, held my breath, and reached in to pull the plug. My hand brushed against something rigid and rough below the surface and I recoiled. The fluid was too thick to see though, so I plunged my hand into the sludge and ripped up the plug.

The bubbling gurgle of rotting body fluids oozed down the drain as I waited to see what was hidden inside. If I weren't leaving it all behind, I'd have been very worried about what it was doing to the plumbing.

Thankfully, the remnants in the tub were not the boy, nor the hitchhiker. It was not even human.

It was the severed leg of a deer that had brushed my hand. The hoof was gnarled and cracked and the leg nothing more than coarse flesh suspended by rotted meat and tendons still clinging to bone.

The muck left behind in the emptied bath was a slurry of torn organ meat and unrendered fat. The rotting dregs of a slaughtered beast. In all my years of cleaning, they had never left *this* kind of evidence. It was always blood, sometimes massive amounts of blood and bile, but never anything that couldn't be drained. I assumed then, that this was left by the boy—or for him.

I did my best to shovel the decaying bits of carcass into a plastic bag and then used old sheets and towels to sop up the puddles of putrid death that remained. I threw all of it into the burn pit out back, then emptied an entire bucket of bleach into the bathroom, just to hide the smell.

Exhausted, I fell asleep on the bed, steeped in the odors of death and cigarette smoke. I dreamt of my sister. For the first time in as long as I could remember, I could see her face again.

When I awoke, it was still the afternoon and the boy had not returned. I was hungry and covered in coagulated filth. I went back to the house and showered in the hottest water I could stand, hoping to burn the odor from my skin. Afterward, I made a sandwich and returned to my perch at the window. I had left the door open to air out the room. I figured that if he had returned while I was occupied, he would have closed it. It was still open.

Night came and I wondered if he had gone ahead, searching for The Family. I decided that I should close the door and lock it. He had left his key on the table, locking himself out, so I'd taken it with me after I cleaned. If he returned and wanted back in, he'd have to ask.

The sound of my shoes shuffling along the concrete walkway echoed off the motel walls. The eerie quiet of the still woods enveloped me. My own breath was the loudest sound I could hear as I approached the open door. The moment my foot stepped past the threshold of the room, I saw his white eyes shrouded in the shadows across from me.

Instinctively, I stepped back, lingering in the doorway.

He hovered outside the open bathroom, motionless and nude. No longer covered in dirt, something else clung to his body. A deep red crust that cracked dry on his skin.

"It was not enough. It rotted," he said from the shadows.

"What are you?" I blurted out.

He waited an eternity to answer, staring at me from across the room.

"You know," he said in a weak, hushed voice.

"I don't."

"You do," he snapped back.

"Is my sister...is she like you?" I asked.

He nodded in a way that seemed he was confused I was even asking.

I stepped backward out of the room. He stepped forward into the faint moonlight shining across the floor. His body was covered in dry blood and his hair was matted in a thick black tangle.

"Please don't hurt me," I muttered.

His eyes grew wide as he approached before stopping. His ghoulish features were suddenly awash in amber headlights. He recoiled into the shadows of the room.

I turned to see the blinding beams of an old pickup truck as it pulled into our parking lot. I glanced back at the boy, but he was gone.

Through clouds of diesel exhaust, the truck rumbled to a stop. The door opened and a tall, sinewy man with close-cropped hair and thick-rimmed glasses stepped out. He wasn't exactly a young man—gray around the temples —but not old by any means. His stature was intimidating, and his voice was deep. His thick meaty hand gripped the side of his door as if he were the only thing keeping it from flying into orbit. A fierce green reflection flickered from his right hand. It was an emerald stone set into a high school class ring, the kind quarterbacks and prom kings wore decades after their glory days were gone.

"Hello," he said, still somewhat hidden behind the bright lights of the truck. A moment of silence hung between us, broken only by the metallic clank of his ring tapping against the car door.

"Can I help you?" I asked, shielding my eyes.

"Sorry," he apologized, then leaned back into the cab and turned off the lights.

I felt trapped between the monster behind me and the stranger approaching from the front. Without realizing it, I had backed myself against the wall.

"You work here?" he asked, noting my retreat, and stepping back himself.

"No vacancies," I shouted, slightly louder than needed.

He looked around the lot and squinted at the darkened motel sign. "Right," he said, before again making that metallic sound of his ring against the steel frame.

"We're uh, closed now. I'm sorry," I said, slightly softer.

"I'd like to stay the night if that's possible, see what this place has to offer. It's been a bit of a drive, and we both know there aren't any options anywhere close."

"We don't have any rooms available," I said, clearing my throat.

"What about that one?" he asked, pointing behind me to the open door.

"It isn't clean," I explained.

"I don't mind," he said, closing the door to his truck. "I can pay in cash if you fancy it."

I shook my head.

"You the owner?" he asked, cocking his head to the side.

"No," I lied. I wanted him to think somebody else knew where I was. That somebody would be checking in on me.

He leaned one hand on the truck.

"None of the rooms are furnished. This one was... but an animal got in and died. I was cleaning it. It wouldn't be sanitary."

"Truly I don't mind," he said, stepping forward into the lights of the motel. His face was hard and serious and altogether unsettling. In all my years of checking in strangers, there was something about this man that seemed different. His insistence to stay was unnerving.

I couldn't help but think back to Gary, about what he said. *This man could be one of them, a killer.* Here I was with my back to a danger I could not comprehend, while in front of me stood a potential serial killer.

He must have read the discomfort on my face.

"Okay, then. Do you mind if I park here for the night, sleep in my truck?" he asked, trying to sound disarming.

I thought about it long and hard. "I don't see why not?" I said, against my better judgment.

He smiled and opened the door to his truck. "Appreciate it," he said, disappointed.

I turned back towards the room, but even with the light from the truck, I could not see inside. I closed the door and locked it. After that, I locked every door I walked through until I was in my bedroom.

Uneasy about the two threats that were sleeping a few hundred feet away, I decided to arm myself. Honestly, I don't like guns and I'd never owned one myself, but my father taught me how to shoot with his. In fact, he taught me with my grandfather's old revolver that had been left to him. The same one that was left to me, still locked in a box beneath my bed. It was my father's lockbox and aside from the gun, I had no idea what I'd find. In my life, all I had been told was not to touch it. Now it was mine.

I had to use a hammer and an old screwdriver to break the lock, but after only a few attempts I was able to pop it open.

The gun sat loosely in the box. Safety was never at the forefront of my father's mind. Beneath it was a pile of important documents, photos, and small mementos that had meant something to my father at some point in his life. Six loose bullets rattled around the steel box like loose teeth in a jar. These bullets were unlike any I'd seen before. The bodies were rugged and each one tipped in shiny polished silver. Though different, they reminded me of the ones Herman had in his box. It was clear these were meant for something more than target shooting. If I had to guess, they were kept as a failsafe or a safety measure in case anything with The Family went...awry. Normal bullets were for intruders; these were for something else entirely.

I loaded the revolver and set it aside. With my task completed, my attention wandered to the other contents of the box. The photos hidden beneath it were not ones I recognized from my childhood. These were all, for some reason or another, private to my father.

The top photograph was of my parents, years before I was born. My aunt stood next to my mother, smiling and holding the hand of a man in his early 30s. I couldn't recall my aunt ever dating and, to my knowledge, I had no uncle, yet the man looked eerily familiar. He reminded me, maybe too much, of The Middle Aged Man in The Family. However, the soft focus on the old faded photo made it impossible to say for sure. He also looked too happy to be the expressionless shell I'd known my whole life. If it was him, it was clear that his life had been hard before he was frozen in perpetual mid-life. That thought alone sent a shiver down my spine.

The photo beneath that one was of my grandfather standing stone-faced in front of the earliest version of the motel. Beside him were four others, who were without a doubt four members of The Family. None of them, my grandfather included, were smiling. To the right of my grandfather stood the older two members of The Family, then The Teenage Girl and The Teenage Boy. The Middle Aged Man and Woman were missing, along with my sister. The photo was old and faded, but even then, it was clear they looked the same as they did only a few days ago.

Beneath that, I found my parent's birth certificates, old bonds, the deed to the motel, and other uninteresting documents of worth. Strangely, I found neither mine nor my sister's birth certificates in their stash. Below everything was a stiff card wrapped in the same paper The Family used to bundle the money, and tied with the same twine. I unwrapped it to reveal the backside of a photograph, newer than the others, with "Chicago, 1984" written in handwriting that was foreign to me. It was not my mother's scrawl or father's chicken scratch. I flipped the photo and felt a cold chill run down my spine. I saw myself, younger than I had ever seen in any family photo. I was dressed in corduroy overalls and standing in front of an old building. The oddest thing, though, was that I was between two vaguely familiar adults, holding their hands. All three of us were smiling. I wish I could say I was able to place their faces, but I could not.

I had to assume they were family friends, but to my knowledge, my parents never had many friends and those they did have would be the ones to visit us. My entire life, my parents made the motel the priority. We had never taken a family trip together outside of a holiday weekend at my Aunt Carol's. As far as I could recall, neither of them had ever mentioned visiting Chicago. They never said anything about seeing friends there, not to me anyway.

Who were these people? Where were my parents? Why wasn't my sister with me?

I couldn't catch my breath as each question came in rapid succession with every frenzied thought. I slammed the box shut. I already had too many questions that seemed impossible to answer. I was not ready for more.

Thankfully, the exhaustion of the day overwhelmed my mind and I drifted off to sleep. The loaded gun sat safely on the nightstand next to me. I had even pushed a chair beneath the knob of my bedroom door. With the heavy curtains pulled closed, the sun never crept in, and I slept until very late in the morning.

Even before coffee, I made my way out to the parking lot where the fog drifted through in such a strange way, it almost looked like smoke. The truck, however, was already gone. I started to feel a twinge of guilt for judging the strange man. That guilt would only deepen as the day progressed.

I opened the door to The Teenage Boy's room and the morning sun flooded in, casting away any dark corners. Immediately, the smell of iron stung my nose. As I walked to the bathroom door, my feet squished into the soaking-wet carpet.

The door was unlocked, and as I opened it, I heard the familiar slosh of coagulated blood being squelched aside. I stepped into the familiar but no less unsettling sight of a tiled white bathroom coated in crimson blood. I prayed to myself that it was, again, that of an animal, though even that did not sit well with my conscience.

I decided to clean. I needed to be sure that no trace of The Teenage Boy was left behind, just in case somebody else came through unexpectedly. That strange man now made me nervous in an entirely new way.

I was so focused that I forgot to eat. Instead, I went straight to work sopping up the massive amounts of blood. It was only when I was on the floor scrubbing that I noticed some of the blood seep through seams in the tiled floor. Narrow cracks in three straight lines forming a box against the wall. I then noticed that the baseboard beneath the sink had been removed and there were small finger-sized holes in the floor where it met the wall. I crawled across the floor, still slick with blood, and slipped my fingers in. I was able to get underneath and pull up what turned out to be a door or hatch in the floor. As I pulled it open, blood seeped into the crawlspace beneath the bathroom. A crawlspace that, until now, I had no idea existed.

I had no choice but to investigate. It was not large, but it was deep enough to walk through without crawling. It spread maybe fifteen feet in every direction. It was dark, but my phone's flashlight was bright enough to reveal the furthest corner. Thankfully, neither the boy nor the man was anywhere to be seen. The floor beneath me was soft dirt made muddy from the blood that dripped down. The walls appeared to be crafted from old red brick and mortared into place, unlike any other foundation on the property. Words written in an unfamiliar language were carved into the walls and alongside them, eight strange faces had been carved in the stone. Except for one unfamiliar face, each one resembles a member of The Family. Even my sister's carved stone eyes stared back in the dark.

The room smelled of smoke, stale breath, and iron.

I moved further to explore the hidden corners. Strange crystalline rocks were scattered, half-buried around the floor. They looked like the ones you'd find in the now-closed caverns of the national park. The most unsettling aspect was the heaps of soft dirt that were arranged in seven large piles throughout the room. One for each member of The Family. Immediately, the room itself felt heavy with dread. I tripped, falling to the ground. The pain jolted me to my senses. I high-tailed it out of the crawlspace, faster than I had ever moved before. I didn't realize I had been holding my breath until black spots began to cloud my vision.

I left the crawl space as I had found it and replaced the baseboard. I finished cleaning the bathroom and doused everything in bleach, careful to avoid the cracks in the floor.

When I returned to the office I noticed there was a message flashing in red on the front desk phone. I checked immediately, unsure of how long it had gone unnoticed. It was just the first of many. The call was from my lawyer, frantically asking me to reach him.

I dialed and waited; after two rings he answered, out of breath. After a quick exchange of pleasantries, he cut to the chase. He informed me that a buyer for the motel had contacted him through my agent. He had placed a tentative bid but wanted to see what the property was about before committing. Apparently, the odd hours I had been keeping recently meant that I had missed the call from both him and my agent. I suddenly realized the answering machine hadn't been checked since before the family had arrived.

"Expect him to stop by soon if he hasn't already. He's on the road for work, so it could be whenever," he told me.

"Oh..." I said, realizing why the man from last night had asked if I was the owner.

My lawyer then changed the subject, and with a somber tone in his voice, he asked if I had heard from anyone in my family.

"No," I told him. Aside from my aunt, I had no family left anyway.

"Well then, I hate to be the one to tell you this, but your aunt passed a week or so ago," he said, clearly uncomfortable.

"What...what happened?" I asked, expecting anything at this point.

"Uh, well, from what I understand, there was a fire at her property, and everything she possessed perished in it, along with her. Her estate had a little trouble getting in touch with me," he said, stammering over the last part.

"So the business is... gone?" I asked, because she, like my parents, owned a small hospitality spot. While it wasn't a motel, it was what you would consider a bed and breakfast. Honestly, it was less of a business and more of a hobby for her.

"Everything," he confirmed. A small part of me was relieved that I wouldn't be burdened with that place as well.

There was a moment of awkward silence, and I could hear him shuffling through papers on his end of the line.

"Is there anything I need to do? Or are you going to take care of transfers, or estate, or whatever? I mean, other than the property I don't know what I'd want of hers. Hell, even the property, I'm not sure I want to deal with. This place is enough." I chuckled in an awkward moment of levity.

He didn't laugh. Instead, I heard more shuffling.

"That is the strange thing. She left you nothing," he said, rather bluntly.

"That's fine with me, I'd rather not deal with it."

"Well..." he said. "You still may have to. You see, she left everything to your sister."

"How old was her will?" I asked.

"She updated it after your parents passed."

"Oh."

"But, I guess now would be the time to open the envelope they left for her. Might have some answers."

"Oh, okay. I'll do that," I said, already worrying about dealing with it all. It was another thing to add to my already overwhelmed mental state.

The conversation shifted to other aspects of the sale and what I would need to do to prepare for it. All the while, the man from last night was in the back of my mind. In an unexpected turn of events, I found myself hoping he would return.

After the call, I tried to push it out of my mind. The boy was gone and as far as I knew, the man had left in the morning as well. I was alone again, high in the mountains in this isolated motel.

I wasn't hungry, but I fixed myself a drink and decided to take my lawyer's advice. I retrieved the third letter left by my parents.

Carefully I tore open one end. Even folded, I could see through the thin parchment that the message was brief, but it was undeniably written in my mother's handwriting.

It said:

"I fear they are no longer the ones we loved. Burn it down. Burn it all down."

The words rang clear in my head as if my mother were whispering them in my ear, "Burn it all down."

The message was spine-chilling. I wanted nothing more than to be done with it, the motel, and The Family, but there were some things I just couldn't let go of. I started to worry that if I sold the motel, other secrets would be revealed. Dark secrets. Damaging secrets. Sure, I could fill in that pit below their room, but what else was hiding on my family's property? The extent to which my parents went to hide one room made it entirely possible that they were hiding so much more.

The gravity of the situation hit me like a truck. I realized how entangled my parents had become and how deep I had been dragged along with them. However, it was my own refusal to acknowledge the oddities around me as I grew up that made it entirely possible in the first place.

I had no choice but to wait for the potential bid to either go through or fail. Either way, the next steps were out of my control. I could always back out and refuse the offer, but then what? This could be my last chance to unchain myself from the haunted property. I needed to figure out what to do next, but to do that, I needed to know where I was heading.

While I waited for the sale to resolve, I packed up what I could from our old family home. Every photograph of my parents now felt different, less genuine. I realized that each photo with my sister missing must have served as a reminder of what they had done. They built secrets upon secrets to protect the child they gave up. I understand that they may have saved her life, but at what cost? Why sacrifice so much for her, yet so little for me? I felt a tinge of resentment and a slight sting of jealousy.

"Why would they keep so much from me?" I asked out loud to a room of family artifacts and meaningless mementos. Nobody answered. I was alone like I always was, isolated with nothing to keep me busy but the endless cycle of questions churning in my mind.

Two days passed and I waited for either The Teenage Boy or the man in the truck to return. I kept the remaining room clean and put together in case either made their way back. With each day that passed without notice from my lawyer, I felt less confident in the man's return. The boy, however—I couldn't shake the anxious feeling that if he did return, it would not be under good circumstances. In my mind, either one would serve as a catalyst in changing my life forever.

Instead, the first car to pull into my parking lot was that of the local Sheriff, Burt Shemp. Burt was a guy who had failed upward until he found himself stationed here. He was a vain man who always acted like he was from the big city, with more jewelry and rings than I think were allowed for officers on the job. He had a special affinity for all things silver and turquoise.

Bert also had a way of making people feel uncomfortable for even the slightest infringement, reveling in his authority. Between the gaudy jewelry, fake tan, bleached teeth, and hair plugs, there was no mistaking the fact that he wasn't from around here. Weirdly, though, in an effort to seem more "small town" than he actually was, Burt insisted everyone call him Sheriff, even when he wasn't in uniform. Not Sheriff Shemp. Not Mr. Shemp. Not even Burt. He insisted that everyone always address him as just "Sheriff." Needless to say, I was not his biggest fan.

My body tensed and my mind went to the room. I pictured the blood-soaked carpet that I cut but never replaced and the stained wood beneath it. To the trained eye, the evidence was there. Unfortunately, for all his shortcomings, Bert had at one point been very good at his job. Early in his career, he had made national news after solving a high-profile missing persons case. Even though he squandered that success by indulging in a series of questionable activities, all of which led to his relocation up here, at his core he was a man with an eye for detail. He wouldn't fall for my bullshit.

I wondered if I'd tell the truth if I were confronted. Would I try to explain myself? Would I try to explain how I fell into a gruesome cover-up that spanned decades? Was it even a cover-up? Maybe I had nothing to hide. It was true that I knew nothing. Except for the fact that I'd rented rooms to seemingly immortal travelers... and that they somehow acquired gallons of blood without notice. Oh, and for years I also cleaned up after them without question. At least one time I could say for certain it was animal blood, but was one time enough? Unsurprisingly, I began to doubt my composure.

I waited at the open door to the office while "Sheriff" sat in his cruiser for ten minutes or so. I wasn't sure if he saw me or not but, regardless, I held my ground. I noticed, a little too late, the cleaning supplies that I abandoned in the lobby. Right next to them, a few gallons of bleach. At that moment, I started to panic. I needed to get them out of sight. Maybe the kitchen? At least, somewhere less conspicuous.

The cruiser door slammed shut and snapped my attention back to him. Walking away now would be suspicious. I wasn't exactly the best liar, either. A lack of human interaction can do that to you.

As he approached the office, he scanned the surroundings, taking note of the unlit vacancy sign. He turned back and registered the naked windows of each emptied room—

that is, of course, except for The Family's room with its heavy blackout curtains.

"Afternoon," he said with a tip of his hat, lifting it in a way to show off his new hairline.

"What can I do for you?" I asked, as friendly as possible.

He removed his shades and peeked over my shoulder into the lobby. "Wondering if I could have a moment of your time to ask some questions," he said with a smile.

"Regarding?"

"Well..." he turned back to the mostly emptied-out rooms. "You have any guests recently?" he asked.

"Closed down a few weeks back, unfortunately," I said, trying to hide my anxiety.

"That's not what I asked," he said, smiling again, but this time with menace.

"Sorry?" I apologized, worried about what exactly he was fishing for.

"I don't mean to be rude or nothing, but we know Bill Henley was on his way up here a few days back. So says his wife. Just wondering if he made it."

"Sorry, don't know him," I said, hoping to end the conversation there.

"You don't know the man who was fixing on buying your place?" he asked, again looking back at The Family's room.

"Oh, him." *Shit.* I scrambled to keep my composure.

"Yeah. Him," he said, prying for more.

"I, uh, my lawyer handled it all. I didn't meet him," I lied.

"Not even when he stopped here for the night?" he asked, showing his cards.

I swallowed hard. I wanted to tell the truth, but I wasn't ready for what came with it.

"Oh, did he drive a truck?" I asked.

"He did."

"Then yes, I saw it. Parked it over there," I said, foolishly pointing.

The Sheriff turned towards the parking spot, to the room, to my secrets. He took out a notepad and began to write something down.

"But he didn't stay with us. We were closed, so he slept in his car. I think," I stuttered.

"Think?" he asked, looking back at me.

I fumbled over my words. "I didn't see him leave. But yeah, he was here for a bit. If, you know, that truck I saw belonged to him and all."

"It did," he said, putting the notebook away. "Mind if I take a look around?"

"Of course not," I replied, the words tumbling out of my mouth before my mind could stop them.

My eyes lingered on the notebook in his side pocket, wondering what he had written down. He noticed and grunted to get my attention.

"Nice, huh?" he chuckled.

I wasn't sure what he was talking about, and it made me very uncomfortable. "Sorry?"

"The handcuffs," he said, unbuttoning and pulling out the handcuffs stored in his belt, right behind the notebook pocket. "Real beauties, huh?"

They were unusually shiny, like they had never been used, which wouldn't be surprising. I nodded in agreement.

"Paid an Indian fellow in Fulton Pass to coat them. Pure silver. Needless to say, they are *not* standard issue," he said, lowering his sunglasses so that I could see smug eyes. His gaudy silver rings caught the sunlight in a particularly pretentious way.

"Cool..." I lied.

I stepped aside to lead him into the lobby, away from The Family's room. Immediately, he took notice of the cleaning supplies and the bleach.

"Is there a problem? Is the man with the truck, uh... Bill, you said? Is he okay?" I asked, regretting my words almost immediately.

The Sheriff's gaze lingered on the bleach for a very long time. He then turned his attention back to me. I could see his mind working over something.

Suddenly, it felt as if the air in the room shifted. His entire demeanor changed, and I felt an aura of warmth from him.

He shrugged and cracked a smile. "Well, I figure it's gonna be on the news soon anyway, if it ain't already," he chuckled.

"What?" I asked.

"Well, nothing good, that's for sure. That truck you saw, they found it about two hundred miles or so west of here. Off old Route 80."

"All the way out there? What was he doing?" I asked, feigning surprise.

"Well, we don't know. We don't know where he is," he said, his gaze drifting to the knickknacks and photographs.

"Oh. That's not good. I don't like that," I said, truthfully.

"You really ain't gonna like the next part. That buyer of yours has a lot to answer for..."

"Like what?" I asked, cutting him off.

"Well, the body they found in the cab for one. Burnt to a crisp. Abandoned," he said, picking up a photograph of me with my parents.

"I thought you said he was missing. The body ain't him?" I asked, trying to find something to do with my fidgeting hands.

"Too young, too small to be him. Best we can reckon, it's a young man they found. No I.D. John Doe," he said, looking hard at the photo. "These your parents?"

I nodded, still trying to wrap my head around it all.

He looked back at the photo, then back at me. "Biological?" he asked.

"I'm told I look more like my grandparents," I replied.

He smiled and returned the photo. "Any photos of them?"

I shook my head, not wanting to go down that path.

We stood there trapped in a long, awkward silence. I motioned towards the kitchen door behind the front desk.

"Did you still want to look around?" I asked, trying to lead him.

"Naw. Maybe later. Just needed to confirm he stopped here, really," he said, making his way back outside.

I followed, not willing to chance letting him out of my sight.

"Okay. Well, thank you for stopping by, yourself," I said, foolishly.

He paused at the door, acknowledging my awkward statement. Then I saw it again, his mind working. He put his sunglasses back on.

"He was alone here, you said?"

I thought hard. What did I tell him? Did I slip? I couldn't remember.

"I don't know," I answered.

He looked at me as if he could tell I was lying.

"Could have been someone else in the truck. It was dark. Can't say for sure," I stammered.

He nodded in acceptance. For some reason, I nodded back.

"Thank you for your time," he said with a tilt of his hat.

As he drove by the dark curtains hanging in The Family's room, he slowed, making a point to look at them as he passed. The pit in my stomach grew deeper with every slow, torturous second he lingered.

I waited until he was out of sight and then ran back home as fast as I could. As soon as I reached the bathroom, I vomited. My nerves were a tangle of anxiety and guilt. I had a sinking feeling that the body they found belonged to

The Teenage Boy. And what about the man, Bill Henley? It just didn't make sense that he would leave behind evidence of a murder in his own vehicle. If he wasn't with his truck, he was either still alive and on the run or still here. Anxiety pulsed through my body as more bile forced its way out of my mouth, like secrets clawing their way free. A reminder of my own self-destructive denial, floating in the toilet.

There was certainly a lot of blood left in that bathroom, but was it Bill's? From the sheer amount of human fluid, it was clear that whoever left it behind didn't walk out afterward. "Then where was the body?" I wondered aloud.

I suddenly remembered the space beneath the room. In a nearly panicked state, I ran back to the room and ripped open the latch on the floor of the bathroom. As I made my way to the first mound, I could feel the dirt below me change. It wasn't the natural clay soil you'd find digging into the mountainside; instead, it had a gritty sand-like quality to it. When I pushed into the darkened mound, my hand sunk in, absorbed by it. The dirt was dry, and I could almost feel it pull the moisture from my skin. I leaned shoulder-deep into each mound, feeling for any evidence of a body or remains. I found nothing. Not a single drop of blood. Even where the blood had leaked down from the floor, there seemed to be nothing left but dry, sandy earth.

Being down there made my chest feel heavy, and the dry air made it hard to breathe. My body hurt from the unnaturally cold, suffocating atmosphere. Once I was sure there was nothing hiding among the dark sand and scattered crystals, I hurried to the surface.

Still not satisfied, I searched the motel grounds for any sign of him. Growing up there, you would expect me to know the place like the back of my hand, but even after all that time, there were areas that still seemed foreign to me. There were always new secrets revealed every time I looked. I couldn't shake the overwhelming feeling of impending doom. I couldn't ignore all the lies that threatened to come crawling from the shadows, like maggots from a corpse.

Eventually, I wandered past the property line into a clearing. I stood with the sunlight beating down on me, absorbing its warmth. I let the sun wash away the cold air that clung to me from the chamber beneath the room. I began to wonder which came first: their lair or the motel. It finally clicked as to why they always checked out that same small room for such a large family.

It was never about the room itself, but what hid beneath it. The unmade beds suddenly made sense. That cold, empty chamber full of dirt was somehow important to them. I began to wonder if there were other chambers like it. Where did they stay when they weren't at the motel? Then I remembered the Ocean Point Inn. We were just one of many rooms they used, most likely stretching across The Ring of Fire...

I had an epiphany.

The Teenage Boy was on his way to their next stop. Another sanctuary. He must have stolen Bill's truck late in the night. I realized in all my years of knowing The Family,

I had never seen them at any time close to dawn or dusk. They were experts at avoiding the sun. Wherever he was going, he couldn't have been far from his destination. He would never have let himself get caught outside like that, not on purpose. There was a reason they only traveled at night, and maybe his charred corpse was the answer. The questions kept mounting, but the answers remained few and far between.

I had to find their next stop. I had to know if it was anything like the motel. And if it was, how? Why? How many more of those earthen rooms cluttered with crystals and soft dirt were out there?

I had to know how we fit into it all, if for no other reason than to ease the paranoia that threatened to consume me. Surely there had to be a rational explanation. Maybe they *were* hunters, as my father had said. Maybe the cool dark room was nothing more than a dry place to store their meat. Maybe there was a rational medical explanation for their aversion to the daylight. Or maybe...vampires were real, and the world was a far more dangerous place than I had ever imagined.

To acknowledge that meant acknowledging that by living my life, I had participated in their atrocities. For my own sanity, I reassured myself that there was a logical explanation for everything, one that didn't include vampires. I pushed those thoughts back. I was afraid I was becoming paranoid, that all my time in isolation was driving me to the same delusional place as Gary. Part of me needed to escape, to run away, even for just a little while. The other, more rational part of me knew I needed answers once and for all. Either way, getting out of the house would help.

I packed what I could into my small car and locked up the motel. I left a note for the Sheriff in case he returned, but I was vague enough not to make it easy to find me. Hell, I wasn't even sure where I was going, so it wasn't that hard.

Before I left, I made sure to reload my grandfather's gun and slid it into my bag. I didn't feel comfortable using it, but I was more uncomfortable with the thought of needing it and not having it. I placed my bag on the passenger seat, within arm's reach. I took a deep breath and, clutching the steering wheel with both hands, I hit the gas and headed down the mountain.

I wasn't sure what I was looking for, but I was certain if I found anything, I had to be ready. I had a feeling there would be no room for error with what was to come.

The drive was long and made longer by the creeping speed I maintained. I kept an eye out for any building or structure that could hide The Family. This meant driving painfully slow and pulling over every few miles to get a better look at each building I passed. It was a long process of excruciating focus.

The truck was found on an extension of the same road the motel sat on. The two-lane interstate split at the base of the mountain and veered west. It was another dead road. Another long stretch of nothing. Spotting anything would be easy because there was so little to look at.

At one point, not far from where the Sheriff said the truck was found, I saw fresh black tracks of rubber burnt into the asphalt. I could only assume this was left by The

Teenage Boy and the stolen truck. Just beyond the skid marks, past the two-hundred-mile marker, I slowed to a crawl and leaned over my steering wheel. Like a ship cresting on the horizon, an old barn crept into view. There was an ominous quality to it. Flaked paint and splintered wood indicated the ancient composition of the structure. Buildings this old carried secrets. It was in their nature. I knew it had to be there. Whatever I was looking for was hidden within those walls. The barn and the old house that laid beyond it were the only buildings for miles. In fact, these structures didn't even show up on the maps. Aside from them, it was nothing but empty fields and abandoned farmland in every direction.

I pulled slowly onto the old dirt road. The rain had softened it into mud and my tires sunk in alongside older tracks. Those tracks cut a path straight to the barn, but I stopped a good distance away. I cut the engine, stepped out of the car, and pocketed the revolver. The sky overhead was gray and dreary; it made for a dark afternoon. I followed the tracks as they led into the old, rotted barn. The heavy doors were in disrepair, but the oiled hinges swung as if they were new.

Inside, the barn was what you would expect from such an antique structure. Old, brittle hay and rusted equipment were left abandoned and forgotten. Everything looked as if it hadn't been touched in decades, except for a strange metal watering trough in the center of the barn. The sickening realization of its use set in quickly. Familiar dark rings stained the rim. Like the bathtub in their room at the motel, this had been filled with blood. It caked in the cracks and scratches of the rusted metal basin. The wooden floor surrounding the trough was stained from decades of crimson ichor soaking into it.

As I stepped closer, the ground bowed beneath my feet and the wood groaned. I stomped. The hollow echo of an empty chamber could be heard below. I kicked aside the dust and hay to reveal the trap door. There was less effort put into hiding this one, the location itself served as the hiding spot.

In the only area that had already been cleared of dust and debris, I found finger holes in the wood and pulled up. The trap door, same as the one in the motel, groaned open in protest. That familiar scent of smoke, stale breath, and iron wafted up, burning my nostrils. Crude wooden steps led into the abyss below. I pulled the revolver from my pocket, took a deep breath, and climbed down.

This room was smaller than the one below the motel but still very much the same. Odd words alongside distorted wooden faces were again carved into the walls. Wooden retaining walls replaced brick in this more ramshackle construction. The earthen floor was similar, but the mountain earth had been replaced by dark fertile soil. The same gritty dirt was again formed into seven mounds throughout the small room. Above me, the cracks in the floor had been sealed with tar so that no light could pierce through. Using the light from my phone, I scanned the room. The same strange crystalline rocks I found below the motel shone back at me with an odd shimmering glimmer. They were arranged in a pattern I hadn't noticed beneath the motel, placed at equal intervals with one at the head and end of each mound. There were fewer crystals here, but enough to catch my eye. I pulled one out of the dirt and held it in my hand. Soft, dusted salt rubbed off with the slightest touch. It was heavy in my hand, more dense than you would expect from the size. I held it in the light from my phone, dark red and blue mineral veins streaked through the otherwise milky white crystal. It was so dry it felt as if it sucked the moisture from my fingertips. I pocketed the rock and continued into the darkness.

With my gaze fixed on the dead eyes of the carved faces, my foot sunk into an exceptionally soft patch of dirt. Without realizing it, I had stepped into one of the earthen mounds, the one closest to the door. This mound was unlike the rest. The dirt was discolored and dryer than the others. It looked almost...unused. Upon closer inspection, I discovered a fleck of white paper protruding beneath the gray, infertile soil. Hunched over, I dug through the dying mound and uncovered a note written on familiar white paper—familiar because it just so happened to be stationary from our motel, with our name on it.

The note read as follows:

"Father, if you have found your way here, I am sorry. We waited for three days, but the fire burned so hot, The Master said you could not return. I begged her to wait, but the soil grew damp, and we moved on. If you've made it here, you know about the orphan. Our oldest home is in danger. In my slumber, I still feel your presence, so I have hope you will find us soon. Hopefully so, as we have left you a meal in the old farmhouse, far from the road. I hope that it gives you the strength to find us again. — Your son, Matthew"

I left the note where I found it. It was so personal, from father to son, but that meant it couldn't possibly be left for The Teenage Boy... or could it? Nothing about The Family made sense anymore.

The farmhouse in question was, indeed, far from the barn, but I worried that driving up might bring unwanted attention. I walked for nearly a mile through waist-high grass on the untilled soil of dead farmland. This plot of land had been long forgotten by those who settled it.

The house itself was in better condition than the barn, but not by much. It had been lived in recently, but how recently I couldn't be sure. It was far from the highway and provided isolated privacy in the way only rural homes could.

I approached from the side of the house and peered through the dust-covered windows. The décor had a timeless, untethered look, and it was unclear if it had been abandoned for years or the residents just had peculiar taste. Regardless, I saw no signs of movement inside. I thought about entering through the window, but caught myself and did the rational thing. I knocked on the front door. The Family and their car were gone, but I had no idea what waited for me inside. The sunlight warming my shoulders did give me some sense of relative safety. Maybe I'd find others like myself inside, locked in servitude, or maybe I'd find something else entirely.

In the quiet between knocks, I thought I heard a brief flurry of restrained movement somewhere inside the house. My hand went immediately to the revolver.

My voice was knotted and stuck in my throat. I swallowed hard and tried to call out, but my nerves betrayed me and wouldn't allow it. Instead, I reached out for the doorknob and the moment my fingers made contact, the door drifted open. I felt as if I were being invited inside.

My first step slipped as my shoes slid on an old pile of mail. Old bills and junk magazines were stacked from years of neglect. Some were postmarked from as far back as the late '90s. My first instinct about the décor was correct. Thick layers of dust seemed to coat most things in the home, but certain spots had been wiped clean with use. A path in the hallway rug was worn down from more recent footsteps. I followed them to the kitchen. There were dishes in the sink and a box of discontinued cereal on the counter next to an empty glass jug of milk. The power had long ago been shut off and the contents of the fridge had rotted past the state of decay and no longer smelled. The ashtray on the kitchen table, however, was packed full of fresh butts. A single unsmoked cigarette was left next to a matchbook. One thing became obvious: the meal was not left in the kitchen.

"Hello?" I called out, adjusting my grip on the revolver.

A metallic rattle and a pained moan came from somewhere in the other room. I stepped carefully in the direction of the ghastly noise. I could hear a subtle rhythmic tapping coming from behind the door at the end of the hallway.

This distance felt further than the distance from the house to the barn. The long, drawn-out moan seemed to seep from beneath the cracks in the door. With each creaking step across the old floor, I worried that whatever was behind that door might hear me. I removed the gun from my jacket pocket and, with my other hand, carefully opened the door.

The ghoulish noise ceased the moment the door opened, replaced by the squeak of unused hinges. I stepped back and aimed.

It was just a bathroom. The soft blue and Pepto pink tiles were not the horrors I expected on the other side. The pipes beneath the sink let out another ghostly moan as they groaned from disuse. The steady drip of a leaky faucet pitter-pattered behind the shower curtain.

Whether it was the sudden rush of fear and adrenaline or merely the long drive, I suddenly felt the urge to relieve myself. Without thinking, I placed the gun on the sink and sat down.

I only had a moment of relief before I saw the silhouette behind the semi-opaque shower curtain. I pushed on the curtain, thinking it was a trick of the light, but my hand connected with something solid. Before I could stand, the silhouette formed into the figure of a person as it reached out toward me. Pants around my ankles, I struggled to my feet. A withered white hand covered in blood emerged from the shower before I was upright. I tripped and grasped for anything to catch myself. Grabbing hold of the only thing standing between myself and the figure, I gripped the shower curtain.

The curtain tore from the rings and covered me as I fell. Frantically I scrambled out from underneath it, out of the room, and away from the gun.

I pulled my pants up and struggled to my feet. As I stood there, face to face with my attacker, I quickly realized that the thing standing in the old grime-covered bathtub was not actually pursuing me. It wasn't standing at all. Instead, the gaunt figure of a dead man hung suspended above the bathtub, swaying slightly from my push.

The room began to spin. The horror of what was in front of me became clearer with the sound of every wet droplet of blood dripping into the bath below.

This was the meal they had left.

I grabbed the gun and before I knew it, I was already outside. Catching my breath for a moment, I considered my options. I thought about burning it down, but that would only bring attention. I knew nothing about fingerprints, fire, or evidence, and the last thing I wanted to do was get tied to this mess. The safest option was to do nothing. This house had remained hidden for so long, why wouldn't it stay that way? To be safe, I took the shower curtain and wiped down any surface I remembered touching. I locked the door from the inside and closed it.

The walk back to the barn was long and arduous. I replayed the images in my mind over and over and thought back to the bathtub I had cleaned so many times before. The nausea that I had become so accustomed to feeling returned with unwelcome familiarity.

If there was any doubt in my mind before, it had been erased. The Family that I had known my whole life were no longer human. They truly were creatures of the night. They preyed on the weak and drank their blood. It should have been obvious, and maybe it was. Maybe my parents knew all along. They had to. But me, it had only coalesced in my mind after seeing the body. The denial had run dry, and it suddenly became clear.

Every two years, for a week at a time, I had been in the presence of an unearthly evil. They were inhuman, unnatural, and otherworldly. They were vampires.

We were only one stop on their tour of death. They must have had other places like ours, the inn, the barn, close enough to make it in a night's drive. My Aunt Carol lived only a few hours east of us. My memories of visiting her came flooding back. It now made sense. I understood why every time I stepped into the guesthouse behind her home, the cellar door would smell of smoke, stale breath, and iron. Occasionally, I'd catch the aroma of soft lavender.

It seemed now that my Aunt Carol had done what my parents couldn't. That was probably why they'd left her that third letter. They knew that she would be capable of doing what they never could. They had made the deal and tolerated slaughter under their roof, but part of me understood why. Even if they wanted to burn it all down, my sister was still their little girl and she needed a safe place.

White knuckled, I drove home with one thing in mind.

I went straight to the burn pit behind the motel and set fire to the evidence. I stood there watching the plastic shower curtain curl and melt in the flames. This same burn pit had been used so many times by my father. It was always after the visits from The Family. Now, it was a haunting reminder of the evil that my parents had tolerated. The evil they had partaken in, even if only by allowing it to happen on their land. They enabled the monsters I had known as The Family.

I contemplated the horrors that this fire had consumed. Outside the center of the flame, a flicker of light off glass caught my eye. My heart sank with the realization that the faint white clouds of smoke I had recalled seeing the morning after the truck disappeared, had come from this pit. I used a stick to dig through the embers. I found the melted frames of thick-rimmed glasses.

He was never coming back. Bill Henley, the man who was going to purchase my motel and unchain me from its shackles, was gone. Like it or not, this motel was still mine. Now, knowing the true burden of this place and the horrors that had transpired every two years, I realized that selling wouldn't be the easy decision I'd hoped it would be. I wasn't sure I could live with myself knowing that I cursed somebody else in the same way my parents had cursed me.

Over the next few days, I was little more than a ghost haunting the motel grounds. I drifted from room to room, trying to cobble together a purpose. I realized that I was bound to this property. Whether it was an ancient family curse or a legal contract, I was supposed to stay here and maintain it.

Once I fully understood the deal my parents had made to save my sister, I felt compelled to protect her. Even if The Little Girl barely resembled the one I remembered, she was still my sister and it was clear that a horrible fate was thrust upon her. My mother, for all her faults, had done what she could to protect her daughter. I worked over the events in my mind and recounted the visits of The Family. I concluded my parents had made a deal to save my sister as a very last resort. I remember her illness, her withering away before my eyes. She was going to die, it was a fact. But somehow, she didn't. My sister continued living as an eternal child, cursed to walk an ever-evolving earth as she, herself, was frozen in prepubescence.

They had changed her into something else, something inhuman, and I was determined to figure out how. Based on how quickly my mother erased my sister's presence from our home, I assumed that any evidence of her transformation would be impossible to find. I looked for clues in my father's old lock box but found little more than unfamiliar photos and documents no longer relevant. Even here, my sister and any memory of her had been carefully removed—or so I thought.

I believe by accident, my father had saved one very important memento of my sister's brief life. It was neatly folded and most likely forgotten in an early memento that my grandfather had kept. Tucked into the center of the first brochure for the cave system was my sister's last remaining link to the living world: her birth certificate. It slipped from the pages onto my lap.

My heart broke for my parents all over again. The thought that my father had saved this rather than a photo of her was so very sad, but I guess it made sense. Why keep a photo when her face was already frozen in time? I imagined, to my father, this represented the little girl he brought into the world, rather than the one still walking it.

I wondered why, of all places, he chose to hide it in the old brochure. Furthermore, where was my own birth certificate? What kind of antique memento hid my records? Normally, the brochure was the sort of thing my father would have framed in the lobby as part of his "history" display. If not for the hastily scribbled red circle scarring the map, it may have been worth a pretty penny too. Finding nothing else, I closed the box.

After several painful hours of finding nothing, I decided to go straight to the source: The Family's room.

It remained almost untouched by The Family or The Teenage Boy. The bathroom, aside from the blood, was seemingly unused. I knew that they would stack their luggage in the closet, but they never used the dresser or bed. Regardless, I searched it for clues and found nothing. If I was going to learn about them, it would be from that unsettling room below. Fighting every urge in my body to avoid that cursed chamber, I pulled up the trap door and climbed down.

I spent an entire day sifting through the dirt in the space below their room. The soft earth that filled the mounds was changing. The dark earthen mounds began to dry and crumble, except for one. Unlike the mound where I found the note, there was a strange dampness to it. I assumed because it was unlike the other six, this was The Teenage Boy's. The spot was still dark with an oily, moist quality to it, though it seemed to have grown more dry and brittle with every passing day. The salty, crystalline rocks placed near each spot seemed to draw out whatever moisture was in the dirt, drying it into barren, useless dust. They acted like a sponge for whatever secretions had leached into the strange soil.

The crystals themselves were not unique, nor rare by any means. They were the same ones that lined the ceiling and floors in the deepest chambers of the caverns. I remembered them from my childhood visits.

A switch flipped in my brain and a memory came flooding back to me. The memory of what my sister had told me before being ushered off by The Old Man. She said they would leave her in the caves. But why? There had to be a connection, and the only way to find it would be to go down there and look.

While the caves had been closed for almost a year, there was still one park ranger who remained on the premises: my old friend Graham Nellis. After getting that transfer he'd applied for when his parents were sick, he slowly settled into his own secluded life. Much like me, he was drawn back to the mountain by a sense of duty. He had always loved the caves, so even after his parents passed, he remained at that post.

We shared an unspoken bond of isolated companionship. For the most part, we were alone on the mountain, and even more so when the tourism slowed. After we reconnected at my parents' wake, he would sometimes stop by for some of that free lobby coffee I'd offered, but he always insisted on paying. He joked that we were the only coffee shop in town, which was partially true. We would chat and catch up, but with so little going on in our lives, we never had much to say. His visits weren't frequent enough to quell the loneliness, but I was thankful for them, nonetheless.

I hadn't seen him in a few months, but his truck passed regularly as he surveyed the outlying grounds. I could tell he was bored, and I thought I could channel that boredom into an eagerness to help me.

I called ahead, but the line went to an automated recording. It played an apology to potential visitors about the indefinite closure. With few options, I made coffee and filled a thermos for him. I got into my car and drove to the closed lot, parking outside the locked fence. His truck wasn't inside so I knew he was out surveying and would return eventually. I wrote a note on an old, empty envelope asking him to give me a call, then I wrapped it around the thermos of coffee and secured it with a rubber band.

I then made the drive down the mountain to pick up some necessities. The strange feeling of returning to "city life" is a lot like returning to school after being ill. Time just moves differently when you're sick or stuck on a mountain. When you rejoin civilization, everything is essentially the same, but there are small changes here and there. It makes you feel a bit disconnected from reality. There are new buildings where old, familiar ones once stood. Restaurants close or change ownership and become something entirely new. The friendly old guy at the liquor store, or your favorite checkout person, either retires or moved on months ago, all while you have no idea. Minute details betray any sense of familiarity.

I wondered if The Family noticed this sort of change, or was life on their scale somehow different? When the scope of existence lasts decades longer than a normal person, what are the differences between weeks or months? Thinking about what it meant for my sister filled me with a great sense of sadness and pity. I knew that I felt alone in the life I was given, but I could only imagine what it felt like to be her, with no hope of ever changing her circumstances. While I could leave the mountain and join civilization if I chose, it wouldn't be as easy for her to step back into the land of the living. If that was even possible for her to do.

With a car full of groceries, cleaning supplies, and other necessities, I headed back up the mountain and returned home. The phone was already ringing when I opened the office door. I put down the bags and grabbed the receiver.

"Hello?" I answered, omitting the normal greeting about room rates and reservations.

The artificially low voice on the other line pretended not to notice. "Hi, I'd like to make a reservation for the honeymoon suite, the one with the heart-shaped hot tub," he said, trying to hold in a laugh.

I knew it was him. "Graham?" I asked, just in case.

"You got me!" he chuckled.

"I can't believe you remember that." I shook my head.

"I can't believe you actually had it... Unless. Do you still...?"

"God no, that went out with the last remodel. It was hands down, the most disgusting thing I have ever had to clean," I laughed. Unfortunately, it was the truth, too.

"Listen, I got your note and the coffee. Thank you. It's a little too late for a tour today, but we can do it tomorrow, if you're free."

"That works. Yeah."

"What about now?" he asked, hastily.

"What about now? I thought you said tomorrow…"

"Yeah, tour tomorrow, but what about now? I've got a bunch of coffee and an hour to kill, but if I drank it all, I'd be up till midnight. So, any interest in splitting it? You'd be doing me a favor."

"Uhh. Sure. I just have to put some groceries away real quick. But yeah, sure." I checked myself in the mirror, thankful that I always made myself presentable before a trip into town.

"Excellent, I'll be right over."

And with that, he hung up.

I rushed to unload everything before he arrived, but with the caves so close, he pulled in before I got to the cleaning supplies. With the coffee tucked under his arm, he helped me carry in the last of my things. I left the bags out, intending to put them away later, and grabbed my two favorite mugs from the cupboard.

We made small talk at first, about the weather and our lives since our parents had passed. We chatted about how things had changed but somehow stayed the same. We reminisced about high school, or at least the parts we enjoyed about high school. Our conversation flowed naturally from one topic to the next as it became clear we had both craved human interaction of this level. I asked how he liked work and the people he worked with, but he told me that the only other ranger on duty just covered the hours he couldn't. They worked opposite shifts, so most of his days were spent alone, listening to terrestrial radio. At one point I broached the subject of leaving mountain life behind.

"Wouldn't you miss the quiet up here?" he asked as we drank our coffee.

"I can't say for sure because, honestly, I have no real reference point. Outside of college, it's all I've ever known."

"Well, city life is just like college but with less classes and, strangely, more responsibility," he chuckled.

"Even in college, I never really settled into a 'normal life' because I knew I'd just end up returning to the mountain," I reflected, wishing I'd done things differently in my younger years.

I eventually told him about my desire to sell, but I lied about the offers. I also decided to frame the bundles of cash as an inheritance rather than an emergency fund. I was careful, even back in high school, to avoid saying too much about The Family to Graham. We were close, but I didn't really *know* him. I trusted him as a neighbor, but there were secrets about The Family that even mentioning would go beyond the bonds of friendship. In the last few minutes of his break, we returned to the subject of the caves.

"What, uh, what spawned this sudden interest in the caves? Why are you suddenly gunning for a visit? Can't be just boredom," he mused, finishing his coffee.

"Research?" I said, asking myself the same question.

"For what?" he laughed.

I tried to parse out my words so that they didn't make me sound insane. I broached the subject gently. "Have you ever seen anything strange in those caves? Or around them?" I asked.

He cocked his head to the side, confused. "You mean like, visitors? 'Cause some of the city folk we get, yeah, I'd classify as strange for sure."

"No, I mean..." I was going to say supernatural but decided to drop the subject. I figured that asking now wouldn't help, especially without context.

"Mean what?" He prodded.

"Like strange geological stuff. You know? Stalagmites and such."

His face lit up. "Boy, have I ever! You are in for a real adventure tomorrow. I'll take you to some parts they haven't opened to the public since before we were born, some that are still closed off to... *normies*," he said, emphasizing the last word. It was what we used to call people that lived down the mountain, the kids in school who didn't share the same upbringing we had. It made me smile.

"We should do this more often. While we still can. Coffee and stuff."

"We should." He smiled.

"Looks like you aren't taking in any more guests, so... When are you thinking you'll be out, anyway?" he asked, standing to collect himself.

"Hopefully soon, but there are some things keeping me tethered. For now."

After he returned to work, I put everything away. I couldn't shake the feeling of guilt for not sharing with him the true reasons for my request. I felt bad for lying, but at the same time, I didn't know how he would handle something as strange as this. I thought that maybe the next day, if the opportunity presented itself, I could bring it up. Hell, he had grown up on the same strange mountain I had, so I wouldn't put it past him to have seen some weird stuff and kept it to himself, like me.

We were, after all, definitely not normies.

I couldn't sleep that night. I found myself pacing the kitchen for most of the morning. I made a small breakfast and then set about packing a few things for the afternoon. I figured it might be a good idea to bring the old cave brochure from my father's lockbox. That red circle on the map prickled in the back of my mind like an itch I needed to scratch. I slipped the brochure into my bag, along with the crystal I took from the underground chamber.

Too anxious to be at home, I left a little after noon. I had the intention of sitting in my car until it was time to meet Graham, but I pulled up to a closed gate. I decided to park on the dirt road and climb over it, eager to get started.

Graham must have seen me arriving on the security camera because he was already greeting me with a wave as I crossed the parking lot.

"Afternoon, Graham. Sorry I'm early," I shouted on approach.

"No worries, more time for adventuring. Sorry about the gate, though," he laughed, then shielded his eyes from the sun, "You sure you want to waste an afternoon down here with lil' old me?"

"A waste of time would be stewing alone in that musty old motel," I replied good-naturedly.

He chuckled and unlocked the door. "When was the last time you made it here?"

"Years," I sighed. "My folks were still around."

"Ah, well there's a lot to see. The remodel finished right before the shutdown. I've been dying to show somebody around, so I'm glad you're here," he said, opening the door.

We walked into the dimly lit lobby, potent with the smell of new carpet and fresh paint.

"Wait here while I turn everything on," he said, clearly excited to have an audience.

I stood in the darkness for almost a minute before the lights came on with the quiet hum of electric life. The lobby was filled with media displays of the cavern's history. There were photos and stories of opening day with updates for each anniversary. As I waited for Graham to return, I studied the older photos behind the glass case nearest to me. My eyes were drawn to the amber hues among sepia-toned snapshots next to black and white photographs, all of them framed in off-white borders where names and dates were scribbled with care. Old brochures, some like the one my father kept, were displayed with ranger uniform patches from a bygone era. There was also antique equipment that past rangers wore while exploring. Each section told a story of a simpler yet more difficult time. As I sidestepped along the display, I found myself going back in time through the artifacts and photos. I wandered towards the early days and the park's opening. So many of these old artifacts were new to me. Either they weren't displayed when I was a kid, or they just didn't stick with me for one reason or another. There were now photos of some of the people I had read about, early rangers and geologists. Names I hadn't thought of in years were popping back up, now accompanied by restored photos and antique nametags. For a moment I was lost in nostalgia.

Suddenly, the hairs on my neck stood straight. I could feel someone watching me. That uncomfortable feeling drew me toward the display of the park's opening day, calling me over, toward one specific faded photograph. It was *his* gaze that drew me in, staring back from the curled black and white. In the photo, a familiar figure stood at the center of a group of visitors, all of them staring back at me.

But it was the visceral gaze of one park ranger that I could feel, standing out among the others. He was The Old Man from The Family. Those same shark-like eyes were looking back at me through the photo. His glare was locked on the lens of the camera and, in turn, on me. It was hard to discern his age in that old unfocused photo, but as far as I could tell, he looked very much the same as he did to-day. The only difference was that instead of his usual gray three-piece suit, he was wearing a park ranger uniform. Unconsciously, I stepped back, distancing myself from him.

"Ah, you've met Jerry? Quite the stare, right?" Graham said with a laugh, back from turning on the power.

"Jerry?" I asked.

"I mean, we don't actually know his name, but we all call him Jerry. He was one of the first rangers to work in the park. He and his colleagues were responsible for a lot of the early mapping of the cave system. Crazy dudes. This photo and a bunch of other stuff was found locked in an old utility closet. Didn't even know it existed, 'cause it was closed off."

"What kind of *other stuff* did you find?"

Graham smiled at the loaded question. "Mostly old gear and trash. One cool thing was that sign back there."

Tucked into the corner of the display was an old advertisement for "Montgomery's Miracle Cure." The ad boasted that the product could cure death itself. A familiar, oddly shaped bottle with a tattered label sat in front of it.

"Kind of wild actually," he laughed.

"I've seen that bottle before. A guest had one."

"That's nuts. It's a neat bottle, for sure. The sign is a little hard to read, but it claimed to be an elixir that leached out death. Apparently, it used some of the minerals from deep in the caves."

"Why? Were they special?"

"The minerals? Can't see why they would be. It also boasts a natural tincture sourced from a rare beast."

"Okay, *that* is wild."

"The general consensus is that it's bat guano."

"Gross."

"Check it out," he said, leading me over the illustrated map covering the entire wall.

He pointed to a blank spot on the map. "Found it all right there, actually."

Remembering my grandfather's old brochure, I pulled it out to compare it to the current map. The blank tunnel he was pointing to still existed on my grandfather's map.

"Oh, that's cool," he said, gently touching the old brochure.

"It was my father's, maybe my grandfather's," I replied, holding it up for him to get a better look.

"Yeah, they left out a few of the trickier spots on the new maps. They didn't want to entice explorers into places they may not get out of," he said, brushing over the dangerous area he alluded to.

"May not get out of?" I asked.

"Yeah, steep inclines, drop-offs, or just plain tight squeezes. They left those spots off, so the map you see today is just the safest, what we call 'vanilla' trails."

I showed him the red circle at the end of a pathway, one omitted in the modern map. "Any idea why that's circled?"

"That looks like *the gulch* or whatever is past it, at least."

I traced the map with my finger. "What's past it? Wait, what *is* the gulch?"

"Not much to tell. It's one of the steepest descents and is almost impassable without gear or a ladder. Which is a shame really; I hear it's the most beautiful place in the system. It's got very unique veined stalagmites."

"Like this?" I said, pulling the crystalline rock from my pocket.

"You're showing me a federal offense, I hope you know that," he said with a chuckle.

"What?"

"You are literally showing me plundered goods. Where'd you even get it?"

"My grandfather's collection," I said, figuring it was close enough to the truth.

"They were a little more willy-nilly with the rules back then. Everybody was taking tokens and souvenirs. Before the Tucker boy, they kind of let people just roam," he said, pointing at a photo of well-dressed folks climbing a dangerous rock formation.

"What happened to the Tucker boy?" I asked.

"No clue. That was the problem. They looked for him for weeks. He was visiting with his wife and son and went missing...well, right around the gulch, actually. Which is why it's not on the maps anymore," he said with another educational chuckle.

"I thought you said he was a boy."

"Eighteen, but he was already married with a son. Times were different back then."

Graham walked to another glass case, away from the main display. "They've talked about taking this down for the renovation. I mean, it is a little dark," he said, pointing at a display of old missing persons photos spanning the decades of the park's operations.

"I had no idea," I gasped.

"That's him right there. Mr. Tucker himself," he said pointing at a class photo. It was a face I knew all too well. The Teenage Boy from The Family stared back, alive, happier, and with a certain warmth in his eyes that I'd never seen. My head was reeling, struggling to process this new information. The Old Man, The Teenage Boy, and The Little Girl were all people who lived and breathed, had families and a story. They had been to these caves, and they all somehow became creatures that didn't age, living off blood. It still seemed surreal, no matter how much evidence was laid out in front of me.

I needed to find the importance of the caves. I knew they were the common denominator, but why? What did they have to do with this?

I surmised that The Old Man had been down in the caves sometime before Mr. Tucker—The Teenage Boy—disappeared. Somehow, they were connected. Something down there changed them forever. I wondered if it was The Old Man that had started it all, or if maybe the Tucker boy went first. He did, after all, appear the same age as he did in the photo, while The Old Man looked a tad younger. I couldn't be sure though. It was like trying to see through fog; I couldn't see the whole story clearly. I needed to keep looking.

I was transfixed by the photo of The Teenage Boy, but Graham was already moving on.

"Listen, I got nothing on the docket today, so if you want, I can take you close to the gulch. I just gotta get some lights," he said, already on his way to the storage room.

As I waited for his return, I made my way to the elevators that would bring us down into the caverns. The gift shop was located across from them so it would be the first thing visitors would see when they resurfaced. Cheesy t-shirts, postcards, and other junky souvenirs were crammed into the small space. The whole shop seemed designed to frame a bookshelf filled entirely with copies of a history book about the caverns. "Tunneling Through Time" was the name, written in an illustrated font. Curious, I opened the book and flipped through the first few pages.

It was as if The Old Man was haunting me through the photographs. Again, his blank stare caught my eyes, looking out from a full-page staff photo taken inside the largest chamber of the caverns. It was labeled as October 23rd, 1924, one year after opening day. Even in his friendly park ranger uniform, his presence was so chilling I almost missed her, hidden among the other long-dead faces: another member of The Family, unaged yet ancient.

Holding the hand of The Old Man was The Teenage Girl. Again, she looked very much the same, but thinner and more gaunt. This was years before the Tucker boy would disappear in these caves. It had to be The Old Man that was turning them, preying on the weak, and changing them into monsters.

My attention was suddenly stolen by the cluttered clanking of Graham approaching with his gear.

"Did he have a daughter?" I asked, pointing at the photo of The Old Man.

Graham leaned over to give a half-hearted glance. "Like I said, we don't even know his real name," he reiterated with a shrug. He then walked over and hit the button for the elevator. His palpable excitement was doing nothing to soften my growing anxiety over the photographs.

The ride down took longer than I remembered, and my ears popped from the pressure change as we descended deep underground. As soon as the elevator opened into the first chamber, Graham disappeared into the near darkness.

"Wait here," he said, stepping out.

I followed but stopped outside the elevator. The dim emergency lights cast haunting shadows across the cavern walls. It was just enough light for Graham to navigate without his flashlight. I could hear nothing but the sound of his footsteps echoing off the walls and the muffled silence of the stale cavern air.

When he reached his destination, his footsteps ceased and the quiet settled in. To my right, I heard a distant flutter and what sounded to me like a faint screech.

A loud mechanical click signaled the lighting system turning on. It filled even the deepest corners of the cavern with comforting light.

Graham returned and, with a wave, ushered me to follow him.

"Alright, let's start this private tour," he said, heading in the direction of the eerie sounds.

"There's no creaky plumbing down here, is there?" I asked, remembering the sink in the old house.

"Nope. All creaky sounds are natural cave occurrences and mostly harmless," he joked. At least, I hoped it was a joke.

I followed him anyway. I was in too deep, both literally and metaphorically. I had no idea how far underground we were.

The walk through the main chambers and less-traveled paths was long, filled with small talk about the remodeling. Graham lamented the fact that reopening wasn't guaranteed, despite the money they spent. He truly loved the caverns and couldn't see himself doing anything else. This was his home or, at the very least, part of it.

"People would die for this gig. It's the crème de la crème of park service posts. I realize how lucky I am to have it," he said with a tinge of real sadness.

"It's lucky to have you."

He turned with a smile, "Honestly, I'd stay down here forever if I could."

It became obvious that we were reaching the end of the modern map. The lights started to stagger, with longer distances between each one. The fixtures themselves were older than the rest, and some were entirely burnt out, creating breaks of darkness in the already dim caves.

Each time we reached an old iron gate, Graham would search a massive keyring for the one key out of dozens that would open it. Eventually, the lights no longer lit our way, and he switched on the lamps and handed me a helmet.

"I probably should have given you this earlier, but these low ceilings make it a necessity," He said with a sense of exhilaration, practically bouncing on the spot.

I followed behind in a half-crouched position as Graham pointed out interesting geological sites. Most had been hidden from the public for decades. I noticed that some of the cave walls were starting to display dark red and blue mineral veins—the same deposits that appeared on the crystals I had collected from The Family's chamber.

"What's that?" I asked, pointing to rune carvings I recognized from the room below the motel.

"No idea what it says. Old-timey graffiti, I guess. Nothing special," he assured me.

"It's not hieroglyphics?" I asked, slowing down to try and decipher them.

"If you think those are cool, you'll really get a kick out of these," he shouted from ahead.

I hurried my pace to catch up. As I approached him, I noticed he had covered his flashlight with his hand, illuminating it in a red glow.

"Ta-dah!" he said, pulling his hand away and letting the white glow wash over the dark cave wall. Suddenly, I found myself in the presence of dozens of faces all staring back at me. Small carved portraits, varying in skill, lined one wall of the corridor. They were similar to but not quite as refined as the ones of The Family that I found carved beneath the barn and inside the motel chamber. I felt a cold breeze blow by, making the hairs on my neck stand straight.

"What are they?" I asked.

"No clue. Same with the graffiti. I think they had some anthropologists looking at it back in the day, but that was decades ago. Not sure if any scientist types have revisited it recently."

Without much fanfare, Graham moved on, leaving me to stand in the presence of the ancient faces. Once again, I had the feeling I was being watched. I quickly hurried to catch up.

As the ceiling and walls closed in around us with each step, the warm air grew thicker. It felt like it was getting difficult to breathe, and my back was starting to ache from the unnatural, bowed posture. Graham must have sensed my discomfort.

"It opens up a little bit further ahead. We're almost there," he said, trying to reassure me.

He was right, and as soon as we reached the next chamber, the air seemed to grow colder, as well. The floor that, up to this point, had been paved with gripping cement installed decades ago gave way to the cavern's natural floor, a slippery surface that felt very much like loose sandstone.

"I present the gulch," Graham announced, grabbing my jacket to prevent me from passing him.

He switched on a very bright lantern that lit the enormous room. My breath left my lungs as I noticed why he had grabbed me.

The steep drop-off was only a few feet ahead, and it was more of a cliff than an incline.

It dropped twenty or thirty feet into a lower tunnel that led into further darkness.

"How do we get down?" I asked, leaning forward to get a better look.

"We don't. Tour stops here. If either of us so much as sprained an ankle, we're pretty much done for. No cell service, nobody knows we're here, and nobody would come looking for weeks. That level of irresponsibility would cost me my job," he said, finally serious for the first time since we descended into the caves.

He beamed with a sense of pride and we shared a moment of quiet excitement. But that didn't last very long.

A faint cry echoed from the darkness past the gulch, a sound that I will never forget—an eerie reverberation that would forever haunt my nightmares. It was a desperate shriek of something near death, a sound I'd heard only once before as a child. It had been the haunting cry of my childhood cat, run over in the middle of the night but somehow managed to drag its broken body to the spot below my bedroom window. It was a sound that I had buried deep in my psyche and had done my best to forget, until that moment when it echoed back from somewhere deep within the gulch.

"Do bats make it down this far?" I asked, my voice shaky and afraid.

I watched his mind wrestle with the possibilities as he shook his head slowly.

"Then what was that?" I asked.

He turned to me, his eyes wide and afraid. He shook his head again. "Don't know…"

My voice echoed down the cavernous path ahead, and the sound ceased as if hearing me. In those brief moments of silence, when we still shared a doubt that we had heard anything at all, I felt Graham pull my jacket to lead me back out.

But then we heard it.

"You've returned?" asked a voice from the distant darkness. It sounded hollow and ethereal, like an echo without a voice to reflect from.

I could feel Graham's body tense with the acceptance that what we heard was very real and not from our own twisted imaginations.

"What have you brought me?" it called out, vulnerable and afraid.

"Nobody should be down there. How did you get down there?" Graham asked as if he wanted an answer from himself and not the ghostly voice below.

There was a moment where neither spoke, as though both were working out what to say next.

"Who's up there? Please, help me?" it begged, the voice now small and almost childlike, more vulnerable than before.

Graham looked to me, confused by the sudden change in pitch.

The voice answered as if it knew what we were thinking, "It's just me, and I'm so scared and alone. Please help me get out of here."

"I'm a park ranger. I... I can help you," Graham said, and I realized that it was now me holding onto *his jacket*, trying to hold him back.

"Stay where you are," he called out to the childlike voice in the darkness.

He turned to me with a look of defeat or unwanted heroism. "We have to help," he choked out.

"Do we?" I asked as he moved past me to an old metal utility trunk to the right of the room. I pulled him back, pleading for him to be reasonable. "That voice, it... it changed. You heard it. We both did."

"Everything echoes down here. Nothing sounds right... We have to at least see," he said, unconvincingly.

Guilt began to boil up from my gut and I felt the urge to tell him it wasn't safe, but I didn't know where to start. Vampires? An immortal family? The Tucker boy? What would he believe? He barely believed his own ears.

As Graham struggled to find the key that opened the trunk, I peered into the darkness. I was looking for any sign of movement and, for a moment, I thought I saw a small pale form move. It was beyond the edge of the shadows and difficult to make out. I strained to see through the darkness, but my attention was soon taken by the metal groan of the trunk opening.

Graham pulled out a rope ladder attached to the side of the already-secured trunk and dropped it below. The ladder unraveled along the steep incline to the floor.

"I've been trapped. Please come down and help me," the childlike voice said, slowly losing all emotion. The urgency was replaced with a calm sense of command.

My stomach knotted and rose into my throat. I found it difficult to speak. "We should go back. Get help."

Graham looked up at me with fear in his eyes and I could tell he wanted to do just that. I waited for him to tell me, to say out loud that we should run, but instead, the voice responded.

"Please, I don't have long. Please help me," it pleaded.

"There's no time..." Graham said with a subtle regretful quiver in his voice.

I followed as he descended the ladder. My hands grazed the coarse granular texture of the cavern wall. I could feel the moisture being drawn out from my skin. With each labored step, the cold dry air stung my lungs.

By the time I reached the bottom, Graham was already halfway across the gulch with the lantern held high. Somehow, no matter how close he got, the light still seemed to stop at the edge of the shadowy darkness ahead.

"How did you get down here?" Graham asked, walking slowly towards the blackened cavern.

"I've always been down here," replied the voice, its childlike essence giving way to a frightening growl.

At the edge of the darkness, Graham stopped to adjust the lamp. With a trembling hand, he did everything he could to cast more light toward the unseen voice.

A pale white figure close to the ground emerged from the darkness and skittered across the cavern floor. It grabbed Graham by the ankles and pulled him to the ground. The lantern shattered on impact. He had no time to react.

I stood frozen at the bottom of the ladder, my light shining only a few feet in front of me.

"Graham?" I called out.

"Run..." he responded in a gurgled gasping moan.

So I did just that. I ran.

Each labored step felt heavy. I looked over my shoulder and caught brief glimpses of the cavern as my light bounced across the walls. I saw flashes of a red wet mass where Graham had once stood and a pale blur of movement crawling across the floor.

I collided with the cavern wall right next to the ladder, almost losing my lantern.

I climbed faster than I thought possible, skipping rungs with each aching pull as my muscles worked on instinct and adrenaline.

I could hear the cold, wet patter of naked flesh hitting the cavern floor as the pale figure raced toward me. When I reached the top of the ladder, I glanced back. I saw the thing pulling itself across the floor with an unnatural speed. It was moving so fast I couldn't quite make out its true form.

I turned to pull the ladder up, my light cast just far enough to reach the bottom of the gulch. A withered claw-like hand covered in scarlet gore reached out and grabbed the bottom rung. It pulled with an inhuman strength. I braced myself and pulled back. I was locked in a tug-of-war for my life. The creature's one arm was strong enough to counter my entire body weight leaning back with my heels dug into the dirt. If its second claw reached the ladder, I was done for. With every pull, it lurched from the shadows coming within inches of grasping the rung. I could hear its other hand clawing at the sandpaper-like surface of the cavern wall, struggling to gain footing and grab the rung. It was only a matter of time before it succeeded.

I looked to my right, into the open utility trunk. Sitting atop a coil of rope and gear was a silver-coated pickaxe with dry brown rust along the blade.

As I felt myself teetering on the edge of falling, I let go of the rope. I quickly grabbed the pickaxe and in one fluid motion, I swung hard, severing one side of the rope ladder. I heard the creature tumble backward, but it never let go.

Still, it climbed, finally reaching my light. The shriveled torso of a ghost-white child covered in Graham's blood. The creature's true age was hidden behind layers of caked dirt and subterranean grime, but the blood was washing it clean. Its waxy flesh was stretched tight over bone, and its gaunt, emaciated face looked alien. The creature gazed up from below with soulless black eyes like marbles pushed into clay. There was no fear, only hunger.

From its waist hung long strips of withered flesh and mangled bone. What were once its legs now dangled in pieces by dry sinewy tendons. The mangled stumps frantically scraped at the wall every time it reached for a new rung. Realizing how fast it could move with only its arms sent a chill down my spine.

The creature made it halfway up the ladder before I swung again, fraying the remaining side of rope. The creature did not slow, undeterred by my pickaxe.

My mind raced as I considered my next swing, the rope or the creature. I wasn't sure if the next blow would cut the rope, but I was even less sure that I could kill whatever it was that was climbing after me.

I swung.

The rope snapped and the ladder fell below. The creature slid back down the incline, hitting the bottom with a sickening wet thud.

I waited with bated breath as I listened for movement. I called out hopelessly into the darkness. "Graham?"

"He is no more."

I swallowed hard and held my lantern over the edge. As the shadows crept back, they revealed the creature below.

I expected a crumpled broken mess from the fall, but instead, there it was staring up at me, unfazed.

Though its resemblance to a human was slight, I could see aspects of The Family in its emotionless stare and pale waxy skin beneath wet red blood. The naked figure was child-sized, but its limbs and features were distorted, odd, and long, with sharp claws at the end of its fingers. Its bulbous, veiny head held two bulging black eyes with thin lips that barely restrained sharp jagged teeth.

It looked as though it may have been human at one time, but its form was now nothing more than a legless ghoul with dry and withered skin. Its few remaining strands of hair were matted with Graham's blood.

"Will you please help me out?" it asked with a sickening grin.

"Why are you down here?" I cried.

"They took my legs and left me to rot," it said, its shark-like eyes locked on mine.

"Who?"

"I gave her the gift, but she turned on me. I can give you a gift too, if you help me up," it sneered.

"How...?" I asked.

"I will drink from you, and you will drink from me, and when you slumber beneath this salted earth, the rocks will leach out the very essence of death from your being. We can live here together, forever. But each night you will follow me here, and we will die beneath the crystalline earth, only to wake at night, revived by the salted soils," it said, digging its claws into a patch of loose gravelly sand.

"What about the others? Do they come back? The Old Man, the Girl, the others?" I shouted down.

It cocked its head to the side. "No. They stole my land and took it with them, but it spoils quickly up there. Down here, it is always fresh. Always clean," it hissed.

My fingers tightened around the pickaxe.

"What is stopping you from killing me once I help you?" I asked, formulating a plan.

"Solitude. Eternity is meaningless if you are alone."

"What about Graham?" I asked, pointing into the darkness. "Can you bring him back?"

"He is not worthy of the gift. You must choose it. He is nothing more than a meal. Sustenance after a famine. But you, I can smell the gift on you. You know of my children; you know what it means."

"If they are your children, why are you here?" I asked.

"She accepted the gift, and we lived for years, preying on the weak that wandered into our realm. And then *he* arrived and stole her attention from me. When she gave him the gift, he convinced her to leave our home. When I refused to let her go, he took my legs and they left me down here to starve. But as I said, death does not come easy down here. Not for us."

"If I help you, can you make me like you?" I asked, my voice shaky and unsure.

"Yes." It smiled.

I looked down at the silver ax in my hands. I thought back to the silver-tipped bullets in my grandfather's box. I realized the rust was not rust at all, but dry, flakey, ancient blood. He must have known. This pickaxe was here for a reason, coated in shimmering silver and already used once before. I knew what I had to do.

I accepted its offer of eternal life.

I tied off the coiled rope in the box and dropped it down. The creature quickly grabbed hold and pulled itself up. One clawed hand over the other, it climbed as its mangled lower half dangled below.

I stepped back and readied myself.

The creature crested the incline and pulled itself onto my level, as I raised the pickaxe high over my head. The creature looked up.

"Liar!" it screamed.

Quickly, I brought it down on the monster's skull with a sickening crunch.

I let go and the blood-covered ghoul fell forward onto the ground in front of me. Slowly it turned its head, and the black expressionless eyes locked on mine.

"Silly… silver slows but cannot kill us. It brings pain, not death." It smiled, bearing its rows of sharp teeth.

As the creature wrapped its unnaturally long fingers around the handle of the ax, I reached into my pocket.

The creature pulled at the handle, trying to free the pickaxe from its head, too focused to notice what was in my hand.

I lurched forward with the only weapon I had left, the sharp crystalline rock. But the creature was fast and swiped at my feet with incredible quickness, as it had done with Graham.

I fell hard and hit my head on the rocks, but the helmet saved me from an almost certain concussion, or worse.

I was still woozy when the creature climbed on top of me, the pickaxe still embedded in its skull.

With one arm, I tried to fight it back, barely holding the creature by its thin, pulsing neck. It quickly overpowered me, but with my other hand, I gripped the crystalline rock. The creature's face was only inches from mine. As it pushed closer, I closed my eyes and plunged the rock deep into the creature's chest, piercing it like a fork through the flakey crust of a cherry pie.

Almost immediately, the skin around the puncture withered and cracked as the rock leeched the life from the creature. I pushed it off and crawled backward.

The creature's blank stare gave way to true horror as it looked down at the fatal piercing blow. Confused, its hands weakly clawed at the embedded stone.

I'd be lying if I said I didn't revel in its death. The creature had taken from me my only friend up on this lonely, death-ridden mountain. Killing it brought some solace. I felt powerful. As it took its final, rasping breath, I felt a change in the energy of the room. I felt a sudden emptiness. The powerful, oppressive force was gone. Everything felt lighter.

I stood up and removed the ax from its skull. Again, I raised it high and then brought it down with a sucking thump, piercing the skull a second time. I swung again, reveling in the gulping crunch of revenge. I swung again.

And again.

And again.

On my final swing, the skull collapsed entirely beneath the blow. Its flesh crumbled in decay until nothing but dust and blood sat before me, soaking into a sludgy mess.

The creature was dead, but the choking loss I felt over Graham remained in my throat. The deed was done, and I wanted nothing more than to distance myself from the oozing corpse. Confident that I had ended this ancient evil, I got close enough to push the curdled blood and mudded flesh into the gulch below.

Using the tied-off rope to climb back down into the gulch, I had a sudden glimmer of hope. Despite what I saw, part of me was unwilling to take the creature's word that Graham was gone. As I stepped over the creatures melting mass and into the darkness, the ground squished beneath me with the rotting sludge of the monster's innards. I directed the light to my feet and the massive amounts of blood and gore that surrounded them. I stepped carefully, but I was unable to avoid the expanding pool of decaying, bubbling rot. It spread from the creature like a dissolving corpse left for months in the summer sun.

I continued forward and found Graham a few feet into the darkness.

His body was cold, but I could have sworn I felt a pulse. Blood oozed from large gashes in his throat, stomach, and arms. Still, I had to try.

Graham was heavy, but I managed to drag him back to the rope. It was only then that I had the sinking realization that there was no way I could get him out, not on my own. By the time I could find help, he would surely be dead, if he wasn't already, and then I would have to explain why. The creature that inflicted his wounds was now nothing more than blood-soaked dust, which made for a poor explanation. They would ask how I found him, what happened, and how he could have lost so much blood without a jagged rock in sight. These wounds would be impossible to explain.

I stood there watching his blood slowly ooze into the grainy sand beneath. I saw it mix with the discolored sludge of the creature that had killed him. I tried to wipe it off him, but the thick, sticky substance only smeared, clinging to him like crude oil. I began to cry. There was nothing I could do.

After several minutes, or maybe it was an hour, I made peace with my only viable option. I would leave him down there and hope that by the time they found him, it would look like he fell climbing down. I hoped that time and nature would hide his wounds. The ragged flesh would hopefully have decayed, hiding the true nature of his horrific death.

I didn't want my friend to stay down there forever, but long enough to not incriminate me. I knew that he would understand. We both witnessed an unnatural evil. There was no way anybody else would believe it, not without evidence. Unfortunately, that evidence had coagulated into a repulsive muck and seeped into the dirt beneath my friend. It churned into a gruesome slurry that seemed to envelop Graham, mixing with his blood and other fluids. The ground around him was already discolored, but I watched as the sandy surface seemed to draw out the gruesome fluids that pooled beneath his body.

I pulled my crystalline stone from the bloody muck that was once the creature and stuffed it back into my pocket. Somehow, it was already dry.

I said my goodbyes to Graham and fought back more tears. With my last ounce of strength, I pulled myself up the rope, doing what I never could in gym class. My muscles burned and ached, but I made it. After a brief rest, I continued.

It took me hours to find my way back out of the caverns, navigating purely by memory. I encountered numerous dead ends and unfamiliar paths, all unmapped by even my grandfather's brochure. By trial and error and a whole lot of luck, I eventually made it to a familiar path. From there, I retraced my steps back to the large cavern and the elevator.

Back in the gift shop, I cleaned myself up and did my best to remove any evidence that I had visited. I even returned the helmet to the rack after wiping away any trace of blood, just to make sure every piece of equipment was accounted for. I'd watched enough crime scene procedurals to know *that* was necessary. I knew I couldn't wipe away the evidence, but replacing it among the other two hundred identical helmets was easier than trying to hide it.

I was tired and weak by the time I staggered outside into the night. I stumbled to my car and drove home in a daze. I barely remembered crawling into bed, still covered in clumps of filth and dirt.

Too shaken to sleep, I laid awake with the lights on. It wasn't until the sun rose that I finally passed out.

The days that followed were awash in sleepless nights and waking nightmares. I felt heavy with guilt and drowned in sorrow. Graham lost his life because of my foolish actions. Even though it meant the evil creature was finally gone, I couldn't help but wish it were me, not Graham, down there rotting. Waiting to be found.

Sleep-deprived paranoia set in and I couldn't shake the feeling that I was being watched. More than once I thought I heard a guest pull into the parking lot, only to peer out the window to see nothing but rolling fog.

My heart broke over and over for Graham. The guilt over his death pulled at the pit of my stomach like an anchor dropped into a boundless ocean of despair. More than once,

I cried until my face went numb. *Did I know what we were walking into?*

I kept telling myself that I had no idea what was down there, but that was a lie. I knew what The Family was capable of, and I knew they were connected to the caves. What I hadn't known was that I would finally face the consequences of my actions, of ignoring the true danger that they posed.

Truthfully, I did try to stop Graham. I didn't want him to go down there.

I just wish I had tried to be honest with him. I had the chance to explain, but in those terrifying moments, would it have mattered? We'd had seconds to react and he was so determined to help what he thought was a person in trouble. Would decades' worth of unbelievable details about vampires have stopped him? I wish I knew one way or another, but I never would. Instead, I had to live with the fact that I led him to his death. In the days that followed, I would have given anything to see him one more time, alive. I still made a full pot of coffee in case he walked through that door.

Even with Graham's death looming over me, I couldn't forget the unimaginable horror that I faced, no matter how hard I tried. My mind refused to separate the face of my sister from the horrifying creature I had killed in the gulch. When I closed my eyes, I saw her face, only to have her smile warp into the gruesome grin of the pale, legless demon that slaughtered Graham.

Every time I walked past a photograph of my mother, I could almost hear her voice in the back of my head, begging me to save my sister. I wondered how much my parents really knew when they made their agreement. Did they know about the creature in the gulch or the violent nature of The Family? Did it even matter to them? Did they make a pact with the devil so long as it saved their precious daughter's life? The guilt gave way to anger and resentment, all of it over the fact that they left me without answers, burdened with a legacy of mystery.

Three days after the events in the cavern, I was awoken mid-afternoon by knocking at the office door.

I expected to open it to a weary traveler who thought we were still open, but instead I found myself face to face with the Sheriff.

He lowered his sunglasses and cut right to the point. "Mind if I come inside? I got questions, and I have a feeling you might know something."

"Sure," I said, breathless and already worried.

I led him inside the office, and he made his way over to the check-in desk. He pulled out a tablet from under his jacket and set it down.

"You're familiar with Ranger Graham Nellis, yeah?" he asked, his brow furrowed.

I glanced at the full pot of coffee on the lobby counter and nodded. "I am."

"You were with him on Thursday, correct?" he asked, as if I had already admitted to it.

"I, um... With him?" I stumbled.

The Sheriff turned on the tablet and navigated it with a small wireless remote. For some reason, he didn't use the touchscreen.

"We have CCTV footage showing you at the cavern visitor center," he said, fumbling through the menu.

Before I could answer, the video played. I watched myself walking across the parking lot and waving to a smiling, still-living Graham.

"Yes. I brought him coffee. He used to come in often, but it had been a while. So, I stopped by. Is he okay?" I asked, regretting my last question.

The Sheriff cocked his head to the side, questioning me.

"Just coffee?" he pressed.

My brain seemed to shut down, overloaded with the possibilities of what he knew, why he was here, and why he hadn't arrested me yet.

"Well, he showed me around the renovations," I offered.

He nodded, accepting my answer.

"Gotcha," he said, already navigating to another video.

"Is there a problem? Did he get in trouble over it?" I asked, feigning ignorance.

"Well, there is a problem. Not... not that you did anything wrong," he said, in an almost apologetic manner.

He could sense my discomfort and cleared his throat. Before he hit play on the video, he elaborated a bit. "Did he mention anything strange when you met? Did he seem afraid of anybody, anything?"

"No," I lied.

"After you left, he missed his rounds. We believe he slept in the center that evening, which isn't illegal, but not really... professional. He has late nights and early days, I get it. But when he did emerge later that night, well..." he said, hitting play on the small wireless remote.

I watched the grainy video fast-forward until the door to the center opened. The Sheriff then slowed the video, and I watched as Graham staggered out of the visitor's center, covered in blood, alive.

I bit my tongue to hide my surprise.

"Notice that he is possibly impaired," he said, pointing to Graham as he stumbled across the parking lot. "We think he may have hit his head while... well, I don't know." He shrugged, seemingly at a loss for words.

"Is he okay?" I asked, with genuine hope.

Without answering my question, he hit fast forward and asked his own. "Do you recognize this car?"

I watched as the familiar old station wagon of The Family pulled into the parking lot. Once again, my heart sank.

"They, uh, somehow unlocked the gate and let themselves in. Figured they might be locals or something."

I was too shocked to answer.

The crushing realization that The Family had returned, nearly two years too early, felt like a cinder block on my chest.

The Sheriff tapped the screen to fast-forward until they got out of the car. All six of them. The Old Man Jerry, his daughter, my sister, the middle aged couple, and The Old

Woman. Like a pack of wolves, they encircled him as he staggered forward.

"What are they doing?" I choked out.

The Sheriff looked at me with sorrow in his eyes, then back at the screen, letting the footage explain.

I watched as The Family encircled and then pounced on Graham. He fought weakly until they overpowered him, losing his jacket and right boot in the scuffle. But they did not hurt him. Instead, they dragged him to the bed of his truck and tied him down at the ankles and wrists using rope from his cab. His arms and legs were splayed out to each corner of the bed. The two men each held an arm, while both women held his legs. The Teenage Girl watched, with my sister hiding behind her dress.

"Hold on, you don't need to see this..." he stumbled, trying to end the video, but instead fast-forwarding it.

"Oh shit..." He struggled to stop it, dropping the stupid, redundant remote on the floor. With a labored groan, he bent down to retrieve it, but accidentally kicked the damn thing across the room.

I watched as The Family got back in their car and left, leaving Graham exposed in his truck.

I watched as the sun crept across the parking lot as it rose above the trees.

I watched his body ignite the moment the sunrise reached his exposed right foot, with odd blue flames licking at his flesh.

I watched those flames engulf him slowly, starting at the bottom of his feet and working up to his head. The crown of fire burned with such intensity, his eyes, nose, and mouth melted into a ghoulish mask of agony. It kept burning until there was nothing left but a charred corpse.

I had watched my friend die a second time.

"I'm so sorry. You should not have seen that," he stuttered, finally powering down the tablet.

I could feel the tears running down my cheek. I sniffled and wiped them away. There was a moment of silence as he let me process the horrific murder I had witnessed.

"We believe they doused him in an unknown accelerant. We're not sure how, but they burned him alive, like the young man we found in Henley's truck. We just want to know why. Do you recognize them?" he asked, bending down to retrieve the remote from under a chair.

I shook my head in disbelief, but he didn't see. "No," I finally muttered.

"We don't know who they are, but we feel they may be responsible for both deaths..." He trailed off.

I looked up, red-eyed. "Doused him in what? We saw everything; they just tied him up..."

He shrugged. "*Did* we see everything?"

I looked at him with anger in my eyes, furious he had forced me to watch my friend's murder. Realizing he was responsible, the Sheriff eased on the questions and tried to soften the situation.

"Sorry, we just want to catch whoever did this."

"Whoever?" I asked in disbelief. "Isn't it clear? They are!" I blurted, motioning towards the tablet.

"They?" he asked, prodding me for more.

I felt my head spin and asked to sit down. He did his best not to act pushy, but his vibe was inherently aggressive. I think he noticed.

"Sorry, take my card. Call me if you remember anything?"

He held out the card. I took it like a white flag of surrender.

He paused at the doorway, hesitant. "They are still up here. The car was seen yesterday, parked near the Murmur turnout, but they were nowhere to be found. We figure they might have some unfinished business; otherwise, they'd have left by now. I had eyes on their car for a bit, but I can't be everywhere all at once. If they show up, or you see anything, call me?"

I nodded with the horrifying realization that they had returned and I may have been the reason.

He left me there on the couch in the lobby, devastated that I no longer had two years to figure it out. The Family had arrived, and that meant they would be checking in sooner than later. I couldn't help but feel that, somehow, they knew what I had done.

I needed to come up with a plan to keep myself safe and somehow free my sister from their grasp. Instead, all I could do was wonder where they had been sleeping... unless they returned to the cave. If that was the case, they already knew what happened to Graham and how he returned. It also meant they probably knew what had happened to that creature we encountered in the gulch. Which would mean... they also knew I killed it.

Before he let the door close, the Sheriff asked one last thing, back still turned: "You sure you've never seen them before?"

I spoke the only word I could muster.

"No."

They were here. The Family's arrival was inevitable, and there was no way I could escape. Not without my sister. The thought crossed my mind that I could just drive down the mountain and be free, but I quickly buried it. I couldn't live with myself knowing that they were still roaming the earth with my sister in tow. I had let Graham die at the hands of those monsters, and with my sister still in their grasp, I was leaving her to a similar fate. If it was true that they would abandon her in those caves, I had to do something. I had to save her. But first, I would have to save myself.

Unwilling to die in my bed, I decided to wait for them in the office, as I always had. The revolver rested neatly on my lap and the coffee pot brewed in the corner. I considered collecting the crystalline rocks beneath the room. I thought of fashioning some sort of weapon, but I feared they would somehow notice their absence and act before I could. I didn't want to chance it.

I still held the crystal that ended that ravenous fiend in the caverns, but there was no way I could dispatch all of them in the same manner. They were never alone, and I always was.

I sat in the office, plotting their demise and fighting the overwhelming urge to sleep. Every sound made by the gentle breeze brought my attention to the parking lot. Every creaking tree sounded like the rusted suspension of their car. I sat through hours of false alarms raised by the natural sounds of the mountain. Alert, I waited.

It was sometime after midnight when they arrived. Despite the unlit vacancy sign and the empty parking lot, they pulled in as they always did. The ominous creak of their antique vehicle was right at home in the haunting woods. They drifted across the foggy lot and parked right outside their room.

The Middle Aged Man was the first to exit the car, rushing to the room with a restrained urgency. The Middle Aged Woman followed. When they found it locked, both stood at the door. Knowing now how strong they truly were, I half expected them to break it down, but they didn't.

In unison, they turned towards The Old Man as he stepped out of the car. There he was, the park ranger from the photos with the same haunting stare. The three exchanged knowing glances, then turned their attention to the office, to me.

I gripped the revolver tight and watched as The Old Man opened the back door of the station wagon. When he stepped aside, a dark figure emerged. For a moment she appeared as a walking shadow, devoid of light, but the truth was more horrifying than that.

The Teenage Girl, covered head to toe in fresh blood, stepped out into the parking lot of my motel. She stood facing my direction for what seemed like an eternity, waiting for something. Her white eyes stood out from the crimson covering her face. On the other side of the car, The Old Woman emerged and turned in my direction.

I suddenly realized that all of them were looking directly at me.

The Girl moved first. She turned back to the car and reached inside. When she turned back to me, she was carrying my sister, her small white dress standing out against the vibrant red. It was the way she held her in her blood-soaked arms that I could tell this was a threat.

The Old Man broke from the group and walked towards the office. Behind him, they watched. Each haunting look fixed on me.

I took a deep breath and readied myself for what I had to do. As The Old Man approached, he glanced at the sign that hung above the door, "You're always welcome."

He grabbed the knob and turned it, and when he opened the door...

He smiled. It was the same fake smile I'd seen a hundred times. He then removed his hat and entered. His wholesome approach was terrifying.

"Hello, we'd like to rent a room. Please," he said without threat.

I sat there in disarmed shock. I was unsure of what to do next, but my instincts took over.

"Okay," I said, surprising myself. I turned to grab the key hanging behind my desk and once again glimpsed The Teenage Girl. Her eyes locked on me, my sister gripped tightly in her arms.

"Here you go," I said, swallowing the lump in my throat.

He took the key with a polite nod and walked casually out of the office.

I watched him stroll back to The Family, joining them at the car for a brief exchange of words. Together, they headed into the room. With an unnerving sense of normalcy, he opened the door and entered. The rest followed in a straight line, except for The Teenage Girl. She put down my sister, who then ran into the unlit room following the others.

The Teenage Girl remained. She watched me through the window with an unnerving gaze. I only looked away for a moment, but it was long enough for her to disappear. A drowning sense of fear made it clear I was in over my head. I had no idea what they were truly capable of.

Immediately, I reached for the phone. I had lied for too long and had brought pain and despair to everyone around me. I pulled the Sheriff's card from my pocket and dialed. He picked up after one ring.

"Sheriff..." I whispered.

"Ah, you again. Did you happen to remember—"

"They're here," I said, cutting him off.

There was a moment of silence.

"The motel?" he asked.

"Yes. Same room, they are...." The line went dead. I dialed again. No answer.

I gathered my thoughts and tried to work out a plan. I had to figure out a way to separate them from my sister. I needed to get her alone so that we could escape together. Monster or not, she was my only family left. My only hope was that the Sheriff and everyone he was bringing with him were prepared. Regardless, I needed to get her alone.

Unfortunately, I had only gotten as far in my plan as "I need to get her alone" when I heard the roar of the Sheriff's engine in the distance. The red and blue lights flashed across the trees as the cruiser approached at a high speed. I needed to act fast before his armada arrived.

The moment he hit the parking lot, he killed the lights and slowed to a crawl. The Sheriff was alone. That familiar lump formed in my throat. I watched him park far too close to The Family's station wagon. I was worried they would know he was coming, that I wasn't alone. Then again, he was the only other vehicle in the parking lot. There was nowhere to hide.

I went to the door, revolver in hand, and peered out through the window next to it. With one hand on the knob, I waited for him.

He stayed in his car for an uncomfortably long time. His sense of urgency was seemingly lost. I realized he was probably calling in the support he would so badly need.

But I thought wrong. Instead, he opened the door, and with a casual saunter, made his way to The Family's room.

"No..." I said in a hoarse whisper. I opened the door to warn him, but before I could get out a word...

He knocked. He waited only a moment before opening the door himself and stepping inside. Terrified, I wanted nothing more than to go back inside the office, but it was foolish to think anywhere was safe. I stepped into the parking lot with the gun in my hand and crept toward the room. I lingered back by the cars, listening for any sign of a struggle, a signal.

Moments later, that sign came in the form of six loud, staggered gunshots.

BANG! BANG! BANG! BANG! BANG! BANG!!

The shots were followed by silence. I ran, but not in the direction I expected. I ran towards the room. Six shots for the six remaining members of The Family. Foolishly I had hoped he missed the last one.

"Stay where you are!" he yelled from inside the room.

I pushed open the door and stumbled inside. What I found was not the heroic scene of a small-town lawman standing over slain demons. Instead, I found him lying in the corner of the room, bleeding profusely from the gut.

As I took in the sight of him, The Family gently pushed me aside and walked calmly out of the room. They paid no notice to the revolver dangling at my side.

The Old Man tipped his hat and flashed that fake smile as he passed, as if this were nothing out of the ordinary.

"Where are you going? You can't leave now! Stay right there!" the Sheriff shouted through the blood pooling in the corner of his mouth.

BLAM! He fired the gun again, straight into his stomach.

"Now you have to turn me. You have to turn me, now!" he shouted, and with each word, the exertion pushed oozing blood from his wounds.

The Older Woman ignored him as she collected her earrings from the side table and walked out the door. She was followed by The Teenage Girl, now cleaned of blood and changed into a modest dress. Neither acknowledging the dying man in the corner.

"I covered up everything for you! You owe me this!" he whimpered.

The door shut behind them, leaving me standing in the cursed room with this dying man.

"Did you... did you shoot yourself?" I asked.

Frustrated, he waved the gun wildly as blood seeped from his nose, mouth, and multiple bullet holes.

"It seemed like a good idea at the time," he joked, gritting his teeth and laughing through the pain. "I know they need me, but I guess I miscalculated how much."

I looked down at him and couldn't help but feel vindicated in my mistrust.

"Be a doll and call an ambulance, would you?" he said, the color draining from his face.

I pulled out my phone. A look of momentary relief flashed across his face. I started to dial, but then stopped.

"What do you mean, they need you?" I asked my finger hovering over the send button.

Frantic worry set in as he realized why I hesitated.

"Oh, cut the shit, we both know what they are. You don't have to lie anymore. You helped me find them. We both want the same thing, you and I," he sputtered.

"I don't think so. What did you do for them?" I asked.

He laughed in disbelief. "Really? Did you ever wonder what happened to the bodies once they were done with them? The ones they didn't leave on the side of the road for me to handle?"

I shook my head.

"It's your property. It's big, but not that big," he said.

"Where?" I asked, thinking about all the off-limits places my father had restricted us from. Dangerous sinkholes, the old septic tank... the open caves. "My parents would never..." I said, knowing it was a lie.

"Your parents, maybe, but the old couple that ran this place did every damned thing they were asked. And look what it got them."

I shook my head, tears welling in my eyes.

"It got them their little girl back," he said weakly.

I stood over the dying man, my whole world coming down around me. I knew the answers, but I wasn't ready for the truth.

I looked in the direction of the hidden bodies, like I was looking through the wall itself, searching for them.

"The septic," he said, as if he could read my mind. "But you don't want to see that."

He coughed, sputtering blood across his already stained shirt, and I realized how close to death he was. I hit send on the phone.

"Don't bother," he said. "Even if you drove, I'd only make it to Gillis Road."

"Nine-one-one, what's your emergency?" said the voice on the other line.

I tried to answer but the words wouldn't come, stuck in my mouth with uncertainty.

The Sheriff shook his head.

"Sorry, misdial. My apologies. Have a nice night," I said and hung up.

"Do what you will with my body, but without me, they're gonna come looking. And when they do, those monsters will be long gone, and you will be left to clean up and take the blame. You should probably have a plan for that."

"But I didn't do anything... it was all them," I said, choking on my words.

"It's your property. Sort of," he said, pausing as a thought slowly came to him. "It's funny, they need us more than we need them. I've watched them. They can't stay in one place. They need 'clean beds' and, for some reason, people like you provide them. Without you, they are vulnerable when they sleep, and without me, they attract too much attention. Still, they find a way to control us. They don't care if you fear them, they are smarter than that. They only care that you fear death."

I had no words.

I watched as the life slowly drained from his body. I wanted to hold his hand, to comfort him, but my repulsion for what he had done overrode my empathy.

As he faded away, he looked me in the eyes and muttered, "I remember your parents. What a shame... You should never have been left here with...them..." His voice trailed off as his eyes glazed over, and his heart finally stopped.

I rolled him into an old sheet and dragged his body to the cruiser outside. With great effort, I was able to heave his corpse into the back seat. I drove it around to the back of the motel and then returned to clean up the trail of streaked blood that led from the room to the parking lot. I used buckets of warm water from the shower and scrubbed it clean with an old push broom. It was a poor job, but I didn't have time for perfection.

I drove the cruiser along the strange path I had avoided my entire life. For something so close, it was unfamiliar and unsettling.

My father had told me as a child that this place was unsafe, and once I was an adult, he further emphasized the danger of it. This is where he took old, rusted propane tanks that had sat for so long the smell of sulfur had faded into a deadly absence. This is where he disposed of waste that was unfit for the burn pit. He said that if I ever wandered too close, it would cause everlasting harm. At least he was telling the truth about that.

* * *

When I reached the unrecognizable location, I stopped the car. I retrieved the large flashlight from the trunk and continued, looking for any sign of... death.

I saw the rusted white paint of old propane tanks buried halfway beneath a layer of dirt and fallen leaves and walked in that direction.

The smell hit first. The putrid stench of decay was so thick you could taste it. The ground beneath me softened as I neared the trench where an old septic tank once was. It was never used and was removed sometime after I was born. It was a remnant of the dream home my father always promised to build for my mother. Instead, they settled into their macabre routine and lived out their lives in the small cottage attached to the motel. I always thought that my sister's death was the reason the dream was abandoned, but it turns out they just found other uses for the plot.

As my view crested over the ditch, my mind struggled to comprehend the amount of death that had been discarded in front of me. Bodies in various states of decay, most of them years or decades old, stacked without regard for their humanity. Rotted bodies sat atop sun-bleached bones resting on a thick layer of decayed flesh, and on top of it all was poor Bill Henley.

His body was almost unrecognizable, no longer the strong imposing man that stood outside his truck. Now, he was nothing more than a withered white corpse, drained of everything that gave him life. Small incisions covered his legs, arms, belly, and neck. His eyes were now nothing more than deep black sockets. If not for the emerald green glimmer of his gaudy ring, there would still have been some doubt in my mind that it was him. I considered for a moment crawling down to retrieve it, maybe mail it to his family, but something told me Bill would rather it stay with him. I felt a strong, nagging sense of guilt for not warning him, but I figured I still had a chance to make it right. At the very least, I could make sure he would be the last victim of my inaction.

I pulled the Sheriff from the back seat, dragged his body to the pit, and rolled him down. He landed just next to Bill.

As quick as I could, I collected the blood-stained linens and went back and remade the bed with fresh ones, hoping that wherever The Family went, they would be staying there for a while. With my eyes fixed on the parking lot, I carried the sheets over to the nearby burn pit, the one my father rarely used. I lit a match and tossed it onto the soiled sheets.

As I watched the flames consume and burn the bloody sheets, I laughed at the futility of burning evidence when I had a pit of dead bodies a few yards away. What was I trying to hide? In the wake of that epiphany, I formulated a plan. It came so quick and sharp, it felt like I had plucked it, premade, from the ether. I stomped out the burning sheets and smothered the fire. I would need those later. I returned to the cruiser and siphoned most of the gas from the tank, spilling it into a bucket I found nearby. I soaked the sheets and any dry wood I could find, which wasn't much.

I then maneuvered the cruiser to the edge of the grave so the headlights would illuminate the rotting mound of death. I walked across the corpses in search of fat-soaked clothing or anything that would burn. Beneath me, I could hear the old bones snap and crunch under my weight. I listened to the nauseating squish of rotted organs rupturing below. By the time I climbed out, the smells of death and gasoline were indistinguishable.

It didn't matter though. I knew exactly how I was going to dispatch these horrible, soulless creatures that had haunted me my entire life, these vampires that had cursed my family's very existence. In order to bring justice for everyone they hurt, I was going to murder every last member of The Family. Except, of course...

My sister.

Red blood seeped into the clean white towels where the Sheriff took his final breath. It smelled of rusted iron and musty linen.

It was an odd feeling to stand in that empty motel room, where decades of untold carnage had taken place so close to where I spent most of my life. Somehow, it still felt like home.

In all my years of emptying the ashtray and replacing their unused sheets, I never lingered longer than I had to. In the back of my mind, I believe I had always sensed the evil beneath the floorboards. But now, I had all the time in the world to linger. I was waiting for their return.

* * *

It was only an hour or so before sunrise when I heard the familiar rattling shake of their old station wagon pulling into the parking lot. It wasn't unusual for them to return this close to sunrise, but this time it felt different. I couldn't quite put my finger on it, but their conversation outside only reinforced my suspicion. I gathered the towels, stuffed them into my cleaning cart, and did my best to remain small and invisible.

As the car door opened, The Old Man's muffled voice became more clear mid-sentence. "...trouble continues, we could reach out to the Neuri clan for help, but... Do you think that's safe?"

There was the slightest hint of desperation in his voice, and if anyone responded, they didn't do so verbally.

The Old Man was the first to enter. He greeted me with that eerie fake smile, abandoning any emotion he may have displayed outside. The others followed, equally devoid of warmth. I pushed my things aside and waited for my chance to exit. The Teenage Girl entered last, holding the hand of my sister.

They continued about their business as if I wasn't there. Most of them headed to the bathroom where I heard the trap door open to their lair below. It struck me then that I had heard the haunting groan of its hinges many times before, only to attribute it to our ancient plumbing.

The Old Man stayed behind and lit a cigarette and then offered one to The Old Woman. She turned back from the bathroom and joined him at the table.

My sister, on the other hand, immediately turned on the old television. She stood in the center of the room and watched as an old black-and-white western movie began with a shot of the sunrise.

With the older couple paying no attention to me, I leaned in and whispered to her.

"I think you left this," I said, pulling the photo of us from my pocket.

She broke her gaze from the cowboy on the screen and glanced at the photo. She took it from my hand. Her nails were long and unkempt with dark grit underneath them. It was more purple than black and I recalled the time I'd hit my thumb with a hammer. That same plum color collected beneath the nail when the blood had nowhere to go. My father heated up a needle and punctured the nail to release the pressure. The blood oozed out with a quick quiet hiss. It was not dirt under her nails. For a moment, I reconsidered whether or not she could even be saved.

And then she smiled. It was brief and beautiful and something I hadn't been sure she was still capable of until that moment. She was still my sister.

"I have the other half if you want it. With mama and papa in it," I said, looking over at The Old Woman, who only spared me a passing glance.

I lowered my voice even more. "I can bring it to you in a few hours. But you'll have to wake up early."

She looked at the curtains covering the window and the world outside.

I tapped at the backside of the photo and she turned it over. In red ink, I had written the words "If you are alone, I will protect you."

She nodded.

I left and returned to my room. I did my best to sleep for the next few hours, but I was constantly awoken by horribly vivid nightmares that reflected my current maddening reality.

When the alarm went off, I had already been awake for an hour. I crawled out of bed and forced myself to eat something. With such a heavy sense of impending doom, I found it difficult to focus on menial tasks like brushing my teeth.

Too anxious to think about anything else, I checked The Family's room, cracking the door slightly, and peeked in. It was empty except for lingering smoke that danced with the dust in the sunlight. My sister was still asleep beneath the floorboards.

I used this time to walk back out to the septic tank, where I lit the gasoline sheets and fat-soaked clothing in the burn pit. The flames grew high, and I prayed this would burn for at least a few hours. Long enough to be noticed when the time came.

At the edge of the pit, I looked down at the legacy of horror that my family would forever be aligned with. If it were ever discovered, this quaint motel in the mountains would not survive. My grandfather's legacy would no longer end with its demolition, but live on as macabre folklore.

As the corpse-fat-fueled flames danced in the burn pit nearby, it became clear that I was on the precipice of insanity. My plan was little more than a half-baked assumption that I could somehow defeat beings that had lived over three of my lifetimes. But it felt as if I had no other choice. I collected every tank of propane that would fit into the cruiser. Some I dug out from their half-buried resting place, others I dragged from where my father had abandoned them with little effort. I stacked the tanks from floorboards to ceiling in the back seat, with a few more on the passenger side seat and floor.

There was just enough gas left in the tank to make it back to the parking lot. Sputtering on fumes, I was able to coast into a spot near The Family's station wagon. The sun was low in the sky and daylight was waning. I checked the room again, knocking lightly as I entered.

I slipped inside without opening the door wide and found my sister sitting on the bed, shrouded in the darkness of the heavy blackout curtains.

I produced the photograph of my parents from my back pocket and handed it to her.

"Do you still want to leave?" she asked.

"Yes. But I will make sure you are safe. They won't trap you in those caves. I promise."

"They think you changed your mind. Master said you are too afraid to leave this place. She said you are weak and insignificant. She said that you are nothing to fear."

"She's wrong," I said, pulling the comforter from the bed.

The light was low, but it was enough to harm her pale fragile skin. I had seen how quickly it engulfed Graham. I knew how little it took to kill them.

I had my sister lay on the bed and wrapped her in the comforters. I tucked in every corner, swaddling her like a baby, and picked her up. She felt lighter than I expected. I clutched her tight, holding the seams close to my body so they couldn't come undone. I carried her to the office as fast as I could. Once inside, I took her behind the desk and set her down. The window shades were drawn, but she remained covered, hunkered behind the check-in counter.

"Do not move until I return. Do you understand?" I asked.

She nodded.

I sprinted back to the room as fast as my legs would take me. The sun was now setting, and I only had a short time before The Family would wake. I remade the bed with the comforters from next door and smoothed them out, as if they would even notice.

With everything in place, I returned to the cruiser and dragged each tank into the room, one by one. I took the heaviest ones first and opened the valves wide. Some hissed violently, while others were a low breathy whistle. The faded odor of sulfur was faint with age, and I barely noticed the scent. With the last tank open, I sealed the door shut and shoved wet towels at the base.

I set a timer for sundown and hurried back to my sister. I found her huddled beneath the comforter with both photos in hand, holding them together as one. She looked up at me with sad eyes.

"I wish I never had to leave. I miss being a child," she whimpered.

The statement sounded so odd coming from such a young... child.

"Do you remember why you left?" I asked.

She nodded. "Mother said it was the only way. She promised to always be waiting though. She lied."

"She did her best. But people can't wait forever," I said, brushing her hair back.

"We can," she replied, looking up at me with eyes that I only then realized were marbled with deep black veins.

"Why do you visit when you do? Every two years," I asked.

"The road is long, and the further we go from caverns the more we must feed. The more we feed, the more dangerous it gets."

"Why don't you stay here, where it's safe?" I asked.

"We can only stay for as long as the earth allows us. If we stay too long, the soil becomes impure and poisoned, so we must always move. Only in the caverns can we sleep forever."

"Then why not stay in the caverns?" I asked.

"Would you choose a life of eternal darkness and constant hunger?" she replied with the slightest hint of indignance.

"No," I admitted.

"The Master lived in the same dark room for so long; once she escaped with her Papa, she never wanted to stay in one place for long. Before now, we had never stopped, and we've never turned around."

"So why now?" I asked, already knowing the answer.

"We had to return so Master could destroy the betrayer. The man in the green hat," she said with a childish giggle.

My watch alarm beeped in warning; dusk was coming.

"Graham?" I asked.

She leaned in with the intensity of a zealot. "When Uncle Matthew felt his father burn in that truck, so close to the barn house, he begged The Master to come back and seek vengeance. But she refused. She felt that his father, Mr. Tucker, was responsible for his own demise. She wouldn't turn around. Not until she felt The Creator die in the caverns."

"Felt him?"

She smiled. "Yes, we can feel the pain of the ones that made us. It keeps us connected. It keeps us safe. It makes us... family. When we found that your friend, the betrayer, had stolen the gift and killed The Creator, he deserved a painful death. He denied it. He claimed that he awoke, bathed in The Creator's blood and soil, unsure of how he got there. But The Master felt the anger of her creator, the fury of betrayal right before she felt him die. Your friend killed him, then took the gift by mixing his blood and letting the earth cleanse him of mortality."

My watch beeped again. I needed to return to the room, but my sister sensed this and grabbed me by the wrist.

"Graham didn't kill anyone," I said, taken aback by her reveling in his murder.

"But he did! And she let him burn in the sun so that his agony would last. Only The Master decides who lives forever."

"And you?" I asked, my voice quivering in a quiet rage.

"The deal grandfather had with them no longer made sense. Mother and Father were going to leave it all behind... and then I got sick. I was granted the gift in return for a permanent safe haven. This continued our grandfather's arrangement. And that is why our aunty was mad. She expected the gift in return for her services, but there was never an agreement with her."

"Aunt Carol?" I asked, finally putting it together.

"She was refused the gift despite what Uncle Matthew promised her. She had provided a haven for us and he made her the promise, but The Master did not. Giving the gift to Uncle Matthew was the payment for haven, but Aunt Carol did not know. She was never going to get the gift."

My words were caught by the lump in my throat. "So they killed her?"

"No," she said with a devilish grin. "She lit herself on fire and tried to take us with her. She failed, mostly. Mr. Tucker was trapped, but alive."

"I saw him. He came here."

"Of course, he did. Uncle Matthew begged Master to wait for his father, but the boy was buried, and the sun was coming soon. So, we left him there. Master said we do not have room for the weak!" Her eyes were ablaze with righteousness. She leaned in close as if telling a secret, " Really, I think she had just tired of him."

"He died trying to find you," I said, feeling the slightest bit of sorrow for The Teenage Boy, the young father who was lost in those caves almost a century ago.

"I didn't mind. He never cared for me much. He only cared for The Master," she said with disdain.

The pieces fell into place; their relationships to each other had finally come together. The Tucker boy had disappeared as a teenager, lost in the caves but found by The Master, his eternal teenage love.

Eventually, his son found him, but only after he had grown into a middle aged man himself. That man was loved by my aunt. She must have dreamed of an eternal life with him, but the deal he made with The Master did not include Aunt Carol. She had made the deal to protect them because she thought she would one day join him, join them. Why they rejected her though, I would never truly know.

"How old is The Master? The girl?" I demanded.

"Old enough to know this world before it was settled, but still younger than The Creator, who lived here long enough to hate the first men. He could not leave the caves. He could not be trusted."

"They should have stayed down there. In those caves."

"She would have, had Papa not pulled her from the gulch. He saved her from an eternity of darkness and crippled The Creator so that he could not follow. That is why they threaten to leave me there when I misbehave. They know The Creator hungers for company."

"Papa?" My heart hurt for my father. She had never called him that.

She motioned back towards the room. "Mama and Papa. They knew *our family*, the ones before our parents. Mama and Papa know the road. They keep us safe. He keeps us fed..." she said with a flash of hunger behind her eyes.

I pulled my arm from my sister's grasp and stood.

Suddenly, I felt her energy shift, her voice lowered to an almost threatening growl. A switch had been flipped and our dynamic changed. Without explanation, she no longer seemed like a helpless little girl.

"I am hungry," she growled.

The little girl façade seemed to slip and she became agitated and restless, like an addict in need of a fix.

"We will figure something out. We can stop on the way down, maybe at the café you loved..." I trailed off, forgetting for a moment that it was closed. There was no going back.

"I do not hunger for food. I do not feed on death. Papa makes sure we eat fresh, before the scent of rot seeps in. He feeds us at every stop, sometimes twice. But he makes sure nobody ever notices..."

The horror of what she was describing hung heavy over me. I hoped Gary Edward Ballard hadn't gotten too close to the truth.

"That all changes tonight," I said, stepping away from her.

"I remember the day you arrived. *That* was the day that everything changed," she replied.

"You were still a child when I was born," I said, dismissing her manic state.

"Yes, but I remember the day *you arrived here.* Mother found you hiding beneath the bed. Too small to consume and too young to be worthy of notice. They left you orphaned, and Mother took you in," she said with a wicked smile, as if she could taste my pain.

My mind was a lightning storm of memories, locked behind trauma and pain. The photo of myself with those strangers was now clear and at the forefront. I thought back to the coldness my mother had for me, while her warmth for other children was always evident.

"You cried for hours on the bed while Mother and Father cleaned your parents' blood from the carpet. They made me play with you to keep you from screaming.

"I don't remember any of that," I said, my hand on the doorknob.

"Why would you?" she said with an evil, hungry smirk.

I didn't want to believe her, but there was truth in her recollection. The photograph I found proved that. Suddenly, I wondered why the woman who cared enough to save me all those years ago, who took me in as her own, never showed me any real affection.

My sister responded as if reading my mind. "Because every time she looked at you, she was reminded of what she allowed to happen in that room."

Still, something nagged at me, one last thing that didn't make sense. "But why would she agree to it? Before you...

before me. Why? What exactly was the arrangement that our grandfather made with them?"

My sister broke her gaze from mine and looked over at the collection of family photos on the wall. "I don't know. You'd have to ask him that yourself."

The alarm beeped a final alert, and I realized I was out of time.

I sprinted to The Family's room and pulled back the wet towel plugging the gap. No odor escaped, and for a moment I was worried the tanks were already drained. I held the damp towel to my mouth and entered. Still, I smelled nothing, but could almost make out a haziness to the air.

With no choice but to keep moving, I tied the towel around my mouth and grabbed the first two tanks. They were lighter than before, which means they were emptied. *Thanks, dad.*

I hurried as fast as I could, tossing the tanks aimlessly into the parking lot. I made no attempt to hide them, I just needed them out of the room. It was impossible to do quietly, but I did my best to muffle any bumps while keeping the door closed as I entered and exited, limiting the leak.

While it took me a half hour to fill the room, it only took me minutes to empty it of the tanks. My hands bled from cuts inflicted by the rusted metal handles, but I didn't slow down. I felt nothing but the tingling rush of adrenaline. My focus was on the task at hand. In every sense of the word, this truly was a matter of life or death.

On my way out with the final tank, I heard the floor in the bathroom creak. The hatch to their chamber had opened.

Whether it was from inhaling the gas, or lack of oxygen, my head began to spin. As I pushed their door shut, one final time, I saw the bathroom knob turn. The door clicked shut and I locked it, then returned the towel to the crack beneath. Exhausted, I moved a few of the tanks around the corner of the building but quickly abandoned the task when I heard movement inside.

I sprinted to the office and found my sister standing in the center of the room.

"What are you doing?" she asked.

"Keeping you safe," I replied.

"I am safe. She knows you won't hurt me. You can't hurt any of us," she said with a condescending cadence.

Standing in the doorway to the office and blocking my way, my sister stared through me with deep black eyes. I realized she was not the little girl I thought I knew. With each passing moment, I felt the emotional distance between us grow and grow. It was her reveling in the pain of others that made me realize she was more them than me now. She didn't need rescuing from the monsters. She *was* a monster. In more ways than one, she was no longer my sister.

I was gutted. The innocence I perceived was an illusion. She was nothing more than a wolf in a sheep's skin. Despite the childlike veneer, she was still capable of the same gruesome acts the rest of them reveled in. I felt sick to my stomach. The images I rebuilt of our perfect childhood were shattered in an instant and the smell of lavender was forever tainted. Everything I had done up to this point was for nothing. Graham's death was for nothing. I could have left; even before I found the money, I could have walked away from it all. But I stayed. I stayed for her.

Suddenly, an unholy scream erupted from inside The Family's room. The Teenage Girl, The Master, had noticed my sister was gone. I thought for a moment that my plan was unraveling, but The Old Man was stuck in his habits.

The door flew open and The Teenage Girl emerged, beast-like in her anger. But The Old Man was not concerned. Instead, he did as he always did. Sitting at the table inside, he put a cigarette to his lips. He then took the fresh matchbook I had left for him next to the ashtray. I imagined him striking the match to light his last cigarette and I smiled.

The explosion shook the very foundation of the motel. Pictures were thrown from the walls and glass shattered in every direction.

When I looked out at the parking lot, my ears still ringing, I saw The Master lying motionless on the asphalt. She was the one who fell prey to that demon in the caves all those years ago. She was the one who went on to turn others of her own... she was a monster birthed from another monster. But in that moment, she appeared as nothing more than an injured young woman, dying on the asphalt.

I stepped outside, taking it all in. My sister rushed past me, letting out a primal scream as she ran to The Master.

Behind them, the motel room was aflame in a hellish fire. I could hear a loud ghoulish moan above the crackle of embers. The Old Man stumbled out, howling in agony. It was the first time in my life I had seen him experience any kind of pain or suffering. It was strangely unsettling to see him so vulnerable, so weak. His flesh dripped from the bone as the heat melted his skin. The pale white skull of The Old Man was slowly revealed behind blackened flesh as it sloughed off his face. With each step, he left behind charred chunks of melted skin in a smoldering trail of burning gore.

He made it only a few more feet before collapsing into a heap of scorched torment. He struggled to crawl away from the flames, but as he tried, his muscles separated from his body. It looked like what I can only describe as pulled pork.

The building collapsed in on itself, trapping the others inside. Smoke and embers billowed from the holes in the roof. Through blown-out sections of the wall, behind the flickering red flames that engulfed the still-made bed, I caught brief glimpses of blistered arms reaching out of the hatch in the bathroom. White smoke swirled around their cooking flesh. Through the crackling roar of the fire, I could hear their screams as they begged for The Master to save them. With a deep exhale, I felt my shoulders finally relax, confident that The Master could no longer save them. Confident that she was dead.

I was an idiot.

She awoke suddenly and leaped up. Her eyes seemed to darken into black orbs set deep in her skull. The Master let out another blood-curdling scream and ran toward me. She moved slower than The Creator, but still frighteningly fast.

I reached into the back of my pants and pulled out the revolver, and within it, those polished bullets. In one fluid motion, I raised it in front of me, cocked the hammer back, and aimed for center mass. I waited until I was confident I wouldn't miss, and then I exhaled and fired.

The first shot struck her in the shoulder, and it seemed to surprise her, the pain from the silver-tipped bullet. She slowed for a moment, feeling the sting. I watched as my sister felt it too.

The Master bared her sharp teeth and continued on, but I waited to fire. Another shot to her shoulder would be fatal, for me.

I waited until I knew I would not miss.

I waited until she was close enough that I could see my reflection in her black eyes.

I waited until it was almost too late, and I fired.

All six rounds struck her, with the last catching her right between those dead soulless eyes.

She dropped to the ground. I remembered the words of The Creator, the creature that dwelled in the caverns: "Silver cannot kill, it only slows."

I pulled out the same crystalline rock that killed that very creature, the creature that started this nightmare. I approached The Master with caution.

I could hear her rapid short breaths as her body worked to push out the silver-tipped bullets. I rolled her over and raised the crystalline rock above my head, ready to plunge it into her heart.

Blindsided, I was suddenly tumbling across the asphalt.

My sister had tackled me to the ground.

"You cannot kill us!" she screamed, her eyes now full black orbs.

"She is the killer! She is evil! I am your family!" I screamed back.

She showed her teeth and leaned in so close I could feel her cold breath on my neck.

"You. Are. Food," she hissed.

She opened wide and bit down. I could feel her sharp jagged teeth as they pierced my skin, tearing at my flesh.

Instinct took over and my hands moved on their own. I told myself I only meant to hurt her when I plunged the crystalline rock deep into her side.

My sister howled in pain and rolled off me. I saw the strange salted rock do its work as the skin around her wound shriveled, and dried like a week-old scab. I went to pull it out, but she pushed me away and grabbed hold of it herself.

She yanked at the deadly stake piercing into her side, trying to remove the crystalline rock with her rapidly drying hands. Her flesh wrinkled into a soft paper texture. She clawed at the rock, desperate to remove it, but it broke.

The larger part fell to the ground with a dull thud. The rest remained inside her, eating away at her innards. She looked me in the eyes one more time and for a moment, I could see the face of the little girl I once knew.

"I'm sorry." I wept.

She fell to the ground as her ribcage collapsed in on itself. Her skin shriveled and her lips peeled back revealing a gnarled cluster of sharp, discolored teeth. Her eyes popped like grapes in a microwave and the sockets pooled with discolored goo. Her entire body contorted with one final whimper of air escaping her mouth. She was gone, but the disfigured corpse before me was so unfamiliar, so shockingly inhuman, I felt devoid of any true remorse.

I looked back to The Master, but the place where she fell was now a spot of wet blood on the asphalt. I looked frantically for her. The orange flames of the fire illuminated everything and nothing at once. The shadows danced across the parking lot, creating a sort of hellfire camouflage. She was still alive, and I was defenseless. She could be anywhere. I picked up the dull crystalline rock and ran towards the cruiser. I could feel the moisture leech out of my hands as I gripped the rock as tightly as I could.

The explosion had shattered the front window of the cruiser, so I had to work fast. From the front seat, I retrieved the items I'd taken from the Sheriff's body; the silver handcuffs, keys, and his service pistol. The moment the flames glimmered across the handcuffs, I was suddenly thankful for the Sheriff's pretentious obsession with silver.

When I stood up and turned around, she was already there, a silhouette among the backdrop of flames.

I fired the service pistol. The bullet struck her chest, but she did not flinch. Instead, she flashed a ghoulish smile.

There was nowhere to hide, and I knew it was impossible to outrun her. I chose the only safe place I could think of. I threw open the back door to the cruiser and crawled in, though I was careful not to pull it shut.

The Master leaped onto the hood of the car and sneered at me through the metal gate separating the front and back seats.

Slowly she crossed over to the opposite side of the car, her gaze locked on me like the predator she was. I backed against the door, ready to push it open behind me, but even then I knew I couldn't outrun her.

She opened the rear door across from me. Her long clawed nails gripped the metal grate over the window as she pushed the door wide open. Somehow, I knew what she was thinking. I could read it on her face. She was sure that she had me trapped. She was toying with her prey.

The Master moved slowly and deliberately as she crawled into the backseat with me. Her pitch-black eyes swirled with reflections of the fire outside. She smiled and her jagged toothy grin was revealed, dripping with foul-smelling slime.

I waited until she was close enough to kill me, and I taunted her.

"This is what I used to kill your Creator," I said, holding up the broken crystalline rock.

Her emotionless eyes remained fixed on mine, her expression unchanging.

With an inhumane quickness she grabbed hold of my wrist, tight enough to break a bone, but I held the rock as long as I could.

I watched her eyes and waited, desperate for the moment she would break away to glance at the dull rock that killed her creator. Agonizing seconds passed, and for a moment I thought she would never break her gaze from mine. But she did. And I acted.

With my free hand, I slammed the handcuff link onto her wrist as tight as possible. In return, she squeezed my wrist in retribution, and I could hear my bones snap. I dropped the rock and kicked backward.

I tumbled out of the cruiser and into the parking lot, hitting the asphalt with a sickening thud.

She then leaped at me but fell short, unable to break free from the handcuff that I had secured to the metal dividing grate inside. She looked down at her wrist, confused as to how it held. It was then that she noticed the silver-plating digging into her wrist. Black tendrils of irritation spread out from the point of contact like diseased flesh, weakening her.

I kicked the door shut and then ran around the vehicle as she yanked at the handcuffs. I slammed the other door shut. With her free hand, she tried to open the door but found it locked from the outside.

Slowly I stepped away, watching the violent flurry of movement as she struggled to break free from the restraints. She kicked at the metal-grated windows, managing only to dent them. The old rural cruiser was built tough; no corners had been cut when that steel was welded in place.

I backed away, slowly, never losing sight of the frantic young girl as she scrambled to free herself from the restraints. From a distance, I watched the fire burning behind her in the darkness, hidden by the night sky, and I waited for her to die. I was waiting for sunrise to come and purge this world of her evil.

From the backseat of the cruiser, she screamed and threw herself against the windows. I watched her fight for what felt like hours, locked in the back seat. Exhausted, I sat back and let nature take its course. She was strong, but not strong enough to break those silver-coated cuffs. Eventually, she resorted to gnawing off her own hand. Thick black blood spurted from her wound, spraying the glass, and obstructing my view inside. She kicked at the windows, but the metal grates held. It seems that even immortal vampires have their limits. Or maybe she realized that even if she escaped, there was nowhere to go. Dawn had arrived.

As the sun crept over the trees, she stopped fighting. I wasn't sure if she had accepted her death or just expended the last of her murderous will to live.

I expected to hear her scream as the sun took her body, but she didn't. I watched as the flames inside the vehicle licked at the blood-spattered windows and, finally, I knew for certain she was dead.

Just as Graham's body became a charred black husk, so did that of my sister and The Old Man. The Master, though, burned so hot that nothing but dust remained in the back seat of the cruiser.

As I stood over the corpse of what I knew was never really my sister, I realized I was no longer linked to this hellish place. I was free of the tether of the bloodline that kept me here, no longer burdened by a sense of loyalty to a family that was never really mine.

I emptied the safe of the blood money that was meant to maintain the motel forever. The only other thing I took was the photo of me with my real parents. The true weight of what The Family had taken from me bore down with unrelenting despair. Not only had I lost the people who brought me into this world, but I lost the world itself, imprisoned on this mountain and held by a false sense of responsibility. I began to hate the motel and the mountain just as much as I hated The Family.

There wasn't anything that held meaning for me here, not anymore. Even the best memories had been tainted by lies and betrayal. I watched as the flames leapt from room to room and eventually to the office and the cottage itself.

The smoke from the septic tank burn pit still billowed thick, black smoke, and I hoped that, whoever came, it would draw their attention there. I hoped that finding those bodies would bring closure to the families who lost their loved ones to the dead roads.

I hoped that those bodies would be the last.

That tonight, I had ended it.

I hope that after hearing my story, you understand why I did what I did. I hope that if you ever meet a family that seemingly never ages, you will know what they really are. I hope that you will know that whatever they promise, you will never be a part of their family.

I left in their old station wagon with nothing more than a duffle bag of old bills, no longer tied to the motel by a legacy of blood. As I passed the fire engines on the way down the mountain, I had a thought:

The Family may have been able to live forever, but until now, I had never been able to live at all.

ACKNOWLEDGMENTS

This book first began as a short story. Originally, it ended with the narrator's discovery of the photograph left by the Little Girl and the revelation that she was their sister. I was thrilled with the twist that I had come up with and posted the story to a forum for "real" spooky stories. To my surprise, it was a hit, prompting many of the readers to express their excitement for the next part... only, there was no next part. Over the course of a week, I wrote the original novella. Each night I hammered out the next section and posted as quickly as possible so as to not lose the momentum of a growing fan base. This story is a macabre stream of consciousness that could only have happened under those circumstances. With all its faults and grammatical atrocities, I am still proud of that original short story, but I decided to improve on it.

The novel you hold in your hands would never have happened without the incredible support from the following people, which I have decided to thank in chronological order. Rod Blackhurst who in between sending me memes suggested I try posting a short story on the horror subreddit r/nosleep. Without his suggestion, this journey would never have begun. My first critic and first editor Jes Barnes, who politely suggested I proofread my stories before posting them and then offered to be the first eyes on anything I write. This story would have been lost to the vastness of the internet if not for u/LighthouseHorror and his incredible YouTube channel. His haunting narration opened up my story to over a million new readers. Because of his enthusiastic fans and their requests for more, I decided to take a crack at turning that novella into a novel and tying up all the loose ends I left in the original. My beta readers who took the time to read my novel when I thought it was finished (it wasn't) Kristen Egermeier, Julia Stier, Parnell Piano, Chrissie Plisky, and Emily Coalson. A little extra thanks go to Chelsey Petty-Dale for being my constant proofreader and Laura Dale for being not only a beta, but omega reader, and letting me know if any of my changes worked.

I'd like to thank my first editor Kylie Lynne Editorial for her amazing suggestions and keen eye for detail. Angie Reiber was instrumental in helping me put the final touches and finding a few more typos and oopsies. That being said, all errors, typos, plot holes, and general mix-emups are all 100% my bad. Outside of printing these and stapling the pages myself, this is as D.I.Y. as you can get in book publishing. In fact, if you catch any more errors, please let me know so I can fix them on the next run. This also goes out to anyone who helped me out with this and somehow didn't get included in this list. I just had a baby, so please cut me some slack.

The incredible cover art was created by Ryan Duggan. He somehow took my vague directions and uninformed suggestions and produced something that far exceeds anything I could have dreamt up. If you dig the cover art, please check out his website and buy one of his Shitting Dog Calendars. They rule.

It's important that I acknowledge and thank my constant collaborators, James Thornton, Will Volkmann, Josh Williams, Vinh Luong, Roger Biersborn, and Joey Lang, who even if their god-level talents may not have touched this book, have constantly and consistently helped, inspired, and carried me in so many other artistic endeavors.

Lastly, I would like to acknowledge my wife Kristina, who has put up with the midnight clickety-clacks of me typing for a few years now. For all of her unending support and amazing encouragement, at the time of writing this, she made it three pages in before falling asleep, but she has assured me she will finish reading this book one day. **I believe her.**

Danielle G Hale

J. Hunter Richardson is a father, husband, and collector of junk. He grew up a punk in a tiny atomic town just outside Los Angeles where they covered up radiation spills, bulldozed occult communes, and tested rockets that carried us into space. He now channels the high strangeness of his hometown into genre-bending stories about hope, horror, and hilarity.